ELISABET

HAUNTINGS

THE WOODEN GUN

"Val, Val, what do you think you're doing? And where did you get that gun? Oh Lord protect us, if They catch you with that . . ."

"But I only . . ."

Gripping the rabbit and apron in one hand, the other descended like a vice on Val's ear as she pulled and pushed him into the house, slammed the front door and bolted it behind them. She was so nervous she could hardly light the lamp.

"Now then, my lad." She put her hands on her hips, taking in great breaths of air. "WHERE DID YOU GET THAT GUN!"

Other titles in the HAUNTINGS series:

13

ELISABETH BERESFORD

HAUNTINGS

THE WOODEN GUN

Hippo Books
Scholastic Publications Limited
London

Scholastic Publications Ltd,
10 Earlham Street, London WC2H 9RX, UK

Scholastic Inc,
730 Broadway, New York, NY 10003, USA

Scholastic Tab Publications Ltd,
123 Newkirk Road, Richmond Hill,
Ontario L4C 3G5, Canada

Ashton Scholastic Pty Ltd,
P O Box 579, Gosford, New South Wales,
Australia

Ashton Scholastic Ltd,
165 Marua Road, Panmure, Auckland 6,
New Zealand

Text copyright © Elisabeth Beresford

First published by Scholastic Publications Ltd, 1989

ISBN 0 590 76172 2

Made and printed by Cox & Wyman Ltd, Reading, Berks
Typeset by AKM Associates (UK) Ltd, Southall, London

10 9 8 7 6 5 4 3 2 1

To
Eric le Cornu,
who was once the boy
with the wooden gun

CONTENTS

Andy and Kate

Chapter 1

Island of Shadows

The boat wallowed slightly, going sideways into a trough in the dark sea and Kate, who had only been half asleep, woke up completely with a start. She couldn't see anything and for a moment she couldn't think where she was. She was frightened. Then she heard the steady sound of the boat's engines and the slap, slap, slap of waves just below the porthole. And after that a much more familiar sound; her brother Andy mumbling away to himself in his sleep on the bunk bed below hers.

Kate blew out her cheeks and pulled the duvet closer up round her neck. It was warm in the cabin, but she wanted something comforting close to her. She could see small specks of grey light around the edge of the curtains in front of the porthole and slowly the rest of the small cabin came into shadowy light. It was going up and down a bit. And every now and again it rolled from side to side so that the overnight sponge bag, which was looped round a tap on the washbasin, swung backwards and forwards, spun in a circle and then straightened itself out again. It made Kate feel a bit queasy so she looked away.

"Umple dumple, yes, that's it . . ." Andy said from down below. A week ago Kate would have found something to throw at him, but now she was quite glad to hear him. At least that was *normal*. But a week ago everything had been nice and ordinary anyway. The four of them had been planning things for the holidays: a day trip to Alton Towers; an air rally that Dad and Andy had been so keen on; the Kingswood tennis tournament (Kate *knew* that she stood a good chance in the Junior League) and instead of all that . . . Kate's eyes stung.

It had all started with a phone call.

"Hello, can I speak to Mr Tostevin?"

"I'll get him for you."

Looking back, Kate thought that if she'd had any sense she would have said that her father was in Kenya or Australia and put the phone down. Only she hadn't, she'd just gone off calling out.

"Phone for you Dad."

He'd come and smiled, picked it up and, thirty seconds later, the office door was shut. When he finally came out he looked quite different. He had his business face on and he'd walked into the kitchen and then shut that door too. Kate could hear her parents' voices going up and down and then her mother quite clearly.

"Oh, Edward, it's not fair on the children."

". . . chance of a lifetime, especially if you come with me. You know how good you are at these meetings . . ."

And even then Kate hadn't stopped to think that

2

anything was going on. She had just picked up her racquet and gone to play against the garage wall. She was hitting the ball well, right in the middle of the racquet, and it was making a satisfactory thud, thud, thud sound when Andy came out of the house with his usual slouching walk, his hands in his jeans pockets.

"Want to play?"

Andy shook his head. He wasn't as good at games as Kate and there's no joy in being beaten by a sister two years younger than yourself, especially when she's a lot shorter. That made it worse. Andy just avoided falling over his feet, they seemed to be growing ahead of the rest of him at the moment, and leant back against the wall.

"Heard what's happening?" he said.

"No. What?"

"Mum and Dad are going off to the Green Canyon."

Kate gazed at him silently. It sounded like something out of a cowboy film.

"Gulf of Mexico," said Andy, kicking at the ground. "Some big oil meeting. They want Dad there."

"Oh, great," Kate said, getting her second wind. "I've always wanted to go somewhere exciting and far away like that. Wait until I tell . . ."

"Only *we're* not going."

That took a couple of seconds to sink in and then Kate's mouth went right down at the corners.

"Why not? It's not fair. What'll happen to us? What about Alton Towers and . . ."

"*I* don't know. Mum's only just told me. Come on, Dad wants to see us in the kitchen."

Edward Tostevin still had his business face on. It

3

made him look older and serious, rather like a headmaster. Mrs Tostevin was pouring out coffee and then fruit juice. What happened next wasn't so much a row as everybody talking at cross purposes about what *they* wanted. Except for Mrs Tostevin, she just kept quiet and looked a bit miserable. It ended with Mr Tostevin saying rather desperately, "It's high time you two realized that it takes a lot of money to keep up a house like this *and* all your extras at school. It means that I have to work for the money and this meeting in Mexico could be promotion. Now let's be reasonable . . ."

"I don't see *why* we can't come with you," Kate persisted. Andy had gone quiet like his mother by this time. He loathed rows and upsets of any kind, while Kate almost enjoyed them in an odd way.

"Because it's strictly business, that's why. We'll think of some really good holiday alternative for you and Andy."

"I wanted to go to Alton Towers," said Kate for what must have been the dozenth time.

"*Alternative?* Not Aunty Joyce," Andy said in some alarm. Aunty Joyce lived in a large flat in Birmingham and she fussed him, especially as his feet, quite of their own accord, kept tripping over things.

It was then that Mrs Tostevin spoke up for the first time.

"What about your cousin, Mrs La Bott?"

Nobody thought it odd at that time that this, until now unheard of, relation should be called *Mrs* La Bott and not Mary or Jean or something more informal.

"Cousin La Bott," Edward Tostevin said slowly, stopping in his tracks. "Oh, I don't know. Well . . ."

4

He looked across the kitchen at his two children: Kate with her under lip pushed out and a really sullen expression and Andy studying the floor as usual. Then he looked round the pleasant, large kitchen with all its gleaming equipment and beyond that to the well-kept garden with the tennis court and vaguely into his head came a picture of the last time he had seen Cousin La Bott and where she lived. It could hardly be more different than their present surroundings. Probably his cousin's house had changed a bit since he was a boy, but all the same . . .

"Now that's quite an idea, Lucy," he said.

"Who is she really?" asked Andy.

"Where is she?" Kate asked. She and her father were very alike in some ways. She knew when he was up to something and she didn't trust that smile on his face.

"She lives on a small, mysterious island," her father replied. "You're always saying how much you want to travel Kate-o. Well this could be your first chance to move beyond the Kingswood tennis tournament and even Alton Towers."

"We've been to Kenya," Kate said. She knew she was being outmaneouvred but she couldn't see quite how.

"Ah, that was a package tour arranged by the company." He chucked his daughter under the chin. "This will be *quite* different. I'll just go and make a few phone calls. I'll take the coffee with me thanks, Luce."

It was always a good sign with him when he changed his wife's name from Lucy to Luce. It meant he'd won on some deal. And he was very good at winning.

And that was how it happened. Kate and Andy

found their unknown cousin's unknown island on a map and could hardly believe it. It was *tiny*; a mere speck in the English Channel and only a few miles from the Cherbourg peninsular. Kate tried a rear-guard action, but it was no use. Her father had made up his mind and that was it. So a very bewildered week later Kate and Andy had found themselves at a large and busy harbour looking somewhat uneasily at a not very big boat which was surging up and down alarmingly.

"I don't want to go," Kate said, sounding about half her real age.

"Oh yes you do," her father replied, putting his arm round her shoulders and giving her a hug. "You're always talking about adventures, well now you've got one. What do you think, Andy?"

But Andy was looking at the boat and didn't answer. He wasn't worried about the boat trip, although neither he nor Kate had ever been to sea. When they travelled it had always been by car and plane. It was just that somehow it all seemed familiar. He watched the evening sunlight dancing and shimmering on the waves and heard the cries of the swooping seagulls as they flapped and floated over the stern, and the rusty grinding of the crane as it swung a rather battered old car on to the deck.

"Are you sure, Edward?" Mrs Tostevin said. She looked pale and anxious.

"Quite sure, Luce." He put his other arm round his wife. "Look at this from a positive point of view. There's hardly any crime on the island. It's a very healthy place and it'll show them a whole new way of life: open country, wildlife, beaches, cliffs, the harbour, an unknown relation, and all the old . . ."

He stopped suddenly, seeing himself as a boy

6

nearly thirty years ago and remembering for the first time in a long while other things about the island which he had forgotten until now: the great grey fortifications, the remains of gun sites and block houses. He shook his head. Well even in those days such things had been taken over by sand and brambles so by now they would probably have vanished altogether.

Kate had been about to say "boring", but she was already starting to feel homesick and they hadn't even left England. She found herself clinging to her parents. They'd all been parted before, but this was different and she very definitely didn't want to go. She felt like one of the ponies at the Kingswood pony club when a jump was too high for it and it braced its legs and rolled its eyes and shivered. But it wasn't any good. Alone with her mother she might have made a big scene and everything would have been altered, but her father had his granite face on again. So Kate scowled at Andy and kicked his ankle. He didn't even notice, although he did slowly hoist himself on to one foot.

There were other passengers, most of them oldish, but there were also a couple of boys in jeans and heavy looking jerseys. They were suntanned and spoke with an accent which neither Andy nor Kate could follow.

"That weren't no 'guid' then, eh?" one said to the other as they went nimbly up the tilting gangplank.

Kate had to cling to the rail, not liking to look down at the churning grey sea below, but both Mr Tostevin and Andy were sure-footed and at once seemed at home when they were on board.

Everything was very confusing, with passengers and crew hurrying along the narrow gangways while the ship continued to tilt slowly from side to side. The noise of the crane was louder than ever. The tiny cabin, with its bunk beds, washbasin with a top which could be bolted down, chest of drawers and porthole, was extremely crowded with four of them in it and suddenly everybody, even Andy, began to talk at once.

"Remember to write . . ."

"Be polite to Cousin La Bott. She – er – can be a bit fierce, but heart of gold . . ."

"I don't want to go . . ."

"I do," said Andy surprisingly, but nobody was listening to him. And anyway if they had asked him why he couldn't have given an answer because he didn't know himself.

" . . . brush your teeth TWICE a day . . ."

"You've got the phone number where you can reach us at any time of the day or night . . ."

"I don't want to go . . ." It had become a wail.

"Wonder if Chauval is still working for her. My word Cousin La Bott used to make me mind my Ps and Qs. I was as quiet as a choirboy when I stayed with her."

"Better not drink the tap water. It's better to be safe than sorry . . ."

"All ashore that's going ashore."

"Is there any sailing there?" Andy managed to get a word in.

"Yes, a bit. But you be careful, there's a lot of strong currents. *Never* go out on your own. Promise me that."

"All ashore that's going ashore, IF YOU PLEASE."

The Tostevin family became aware that now there were five of them in the tiny cabin. A tall, thin man in a smart uniform was watching them patiently. His face had a battered, but kindly look about it and in a firm, but polite way he got them all out and led them up the narrow gangway and steep steps to the top deck.

"The name's Joe," he said. "Don't fret yourselves, I'll keep an eye on everything. Bit of a swell coming up tonight, so I'll hand round the pills if anybody wants them AND see that they get to their bunks early. The cafeteria's open now. This way IF you please. Excuse me, Madam, thank you, Sir. Name of Tostevin, isn't it? Good old island name. The wife's younger sister is married to a Tostevin."

"Andy and Kate are staying with their grandfather's cousin, Mrs La Bott. Perhaps you know her?"

Joe's blue eyes glinted even more as he slid the coins Mr Tostevin had given him into his pocket. It seemed that he was about to say something and then changed his mind.

"Yes, indeed, Sir," his voice gave nothing away. We *all* know Madame La Bott. If you please now, we're about to sail . . ."

There was no more time, just a last series of hugs and then, quite suddenly, the Tostevin family had been split into two, the parents going down the gangplank which was now at a much sharper angle so that Mr Tostevin had to help his wife. They stood on the quay looking up as the gangplank was rattled on board and the crane swung away as if it was no longer interested in what was going on. There was a very loud blast on the ship's hooter which made everybody jump and sent the seagulls screeching and calling into the darkening sky. The engines were throbbing far below and there was dark smoke coming out of the

9

fat, low funnel as the anchors rattled on board and the boat began to edge out away from the quay and then, somewhat surprisingly, started to steam backward towards the middle of the harbour.

The land seemed to fall away and become suddenly darker so that they could see the headlamps of cars moving very slowly, but at sea it was still only dusk and then they were beyond the comforting arm of the harbour wall and the ship bounced as the helmsman brought her round so that the bow was facing south and out to sea. Kate hit the rails quite hard. She was both scared and a little hurt and she would have liked to have burst into extremely loud tears, but Joe stopped her.

"Down we go," he said firmly. "What you need is something to quieten your stomach." And he led her off with Andy, for once not falling over his feet, following along behind.

The rest of the evening was a blur. Neither of them was sick, but a couple of slices of toast and Marmite seemed quite enough to eat and, once they were in their cabin and had learnt very quickly *not* to put too much water in the washbasin as in two seconds flat it was washing their feet, the only sensible thing to do was to go to bed. They were asleep within two minutes.

All this went in and out of Kate's head now, and she suddenly felt extremely homesick for all the usual things of home: Radio Two being played in the kitchen; the steady swish, swish of cars on the road beyond the front garden; her mother calling out for the sixth time that breakfast was ready; the slurp of mail coming through the letterbox and a thousand other things. Even Dad roaring at Andy NOT TO LEAVE HIS BIKE ON THE GRASS ALL

NIGHT AGAIN, would have been welcome. But now there was nothing but the rumble of the ship's engines and the slapping of the waves. Even Andy had quietened down.

Kate hung out from her bunk and jerked back the orange curtains, screwing up her eyes against the very bright sunlight which was sparkling back at her from the waves. A gull careened past and made her pull back. It was a very large bird. And beyond the waves was a bumpy dark outline which was rapidly getting larger. It was almost mountainous with its cliffs climbing upwards out of the sea. And on the cliff top itself was a building like a long castle; then a lighthouse, more cliffs, a few houses, a big curving beach backed up by a lot of rocks, a grim great grey building with enormous empty windows so that it looked like a gigantic skull, a few more houses, another beach with fortresses at either end . . .

It was like watching a television picture as all this slowly flowed past the porthole. The sun was fully up now, the last of the sunrise red skipping across the waves and then vanishing, so the island was bathed in a golden glow. Kate went on gazing at it, unable to look away. It was like nothing she had ever seen before and it was beautiful. But not to her.

Kate shivered and hauled the duvet round her as the harbour and then a small town behind it came into view. Because in spite of the sunshine, to her it was as if some great shadow hung over everything she could see. She knew it wasn't there, but somehow in some strange way she could feel it.

"Umble, crumble. What?" said Andy, waking up instantly.

Chapter 2

The Accident

"What do you mean you don't like it?" Andy said. He was hunched over the rail, his eyes on the fast-approaching harbour wall. They seemed to be going a very long way round the end of it before turning to come in shore.

"Here, I've brought you some sandwiches." Joe came up behind them, a plate balanced neatly on his spread fingers, his knees flexing easily to counteract the motion of the boat. "The island'll give you an appetite like you've never had before, I'm telling you."

"That's very kind of you," Kate said thickly. She didn't want any sandwiches. There was a lump of pure misery in her throat and she would have given everything she had in the world to be back in the Kingswood kitchen. But she took a sandwich and nibbled it, trying not to feel sick. Perhaps in a moment when Joe had gone below she could feed it to a passing seabird. Andy took two and had an enormous mouthful. His spirits were the exact opposite to Kate's: they were going up and up. It was like the night before when he'd first seen the boat, it was all so familiar, so *right* somehow, as though he and the island had been waiting for each other. He said even more thickly than Kate, "Why are we turning in such a large circle?" Only it came out as "shirkle".

"Because we have to clear the old harbour wall. There was a – oh, trouble on the island, and then a big storm brought the rest of it down a long time ago. The remains are still there on the sea bed though and the tide's at slack water at the moment, so it's better to be safe than sorry with a large hole in your beam."

They strained forward over the rail. And under the choppy glinting water they could, perhaps, see large dark shadows. But now they were turning towards the land. To the left there was an enormous fort on top of a headland and then curving high land covered in grass and brambles which came down to a road and then a long beach with sand and a few rocks. Underneath the fort Andy could see a water skier being pulled along by a small, fast boat and his spirits rose even more. Probably having big feet would be an advantage in a sport like that.

A faint nudge in the ribs made him turn to look at Kate. Her face was very pale and she was offering him her barely nibbled sandwich.

"Thanks, we'll be on land in a tick," Andy said, devouring it. He thought she was pale because of sea sickness. Quite carried away because he felt so happy and excited himself, he put his arm round her. And instead of telling him to "push off" or snapping at him, Kate actually stood still, shivering a little. They

13

were coming in fast now and they could see an inner harbour with bobbing fishing boats packed side by side with large, brightly coloured buoys tied to their rails looking like enormous balloons. There were some houses along the edge of the beach and a few more straggling up the hill to the right, but what struck Andy was the lack of traffic. One old van was slowly going up the hill road and there was a motorbike skimming along the coast road and that was it. They had slowed right down by now as they edged into their berth.

"Best get your things together," Joe said. "Once we're tied up alongside you'll be put ashore quite sharp."

He was right for as they reappeared on the deck the elderly passengers and the two boys were already away and the crane, another one given to screeching, was unloading cargo.

"Thanks and all that," Andy said, shaking Joe's hand.

"Say Joe send his regards to Madame La Bott." Again that smile flitted across Joe's grizzled face, as though he knew some secret joke. Kate couldn't speak for the life of her. It was back again, that feeling of being frightened of something she couldn't see, but could only feel.

"There she is now," Joe gestured down to the dock. Andy stared incredulously. She was *tiny*; an elderly woman with grey hair drawn straight back off her face and into a bun; a belted raincoat, her hands clasped in front of her. She was watching them intently and then one small hand was raised in greeting. Once they had clambered down the gang-plank and were face to face with her she seemed smaller than ever and Andy had never felt so large nor

14

so clumsy. Everything about Madame La Bott was neat and precise. She inclined her head and held out her hand. She had a surprisingly strong grip.

"So you'll be Andrew and Katherine. Welcome to the island. You can call me Cousin La Bott, there's no need for all this Madame nonsense, seeing as we're related even if distantly. Yes I can see the likeness to your father. How is he?"

"Fine, thanks," said Andy. He was fascinated by her. Somehow it was as if she and the island were very like each other. Kate still couldn't speak. If she did she would burst into tears. Cousin La Bott's sharp grey eyes considered her, but she only said, "Well come along, the car's along by the chippy. I'll take the little bag, you can manage the rest between you, eh?"

She too had the strange accent of the boys on the boat, but it wasn't so pronounced and Andy could easily understand her. Kate just didn't notice anything as she trailed along behind them. Andy took a deep breath as they went past the chippy, it was one of his favourite smells in the world after grilling bacon and hot garlic bread. The small quay was quite busy, but everyone, even the toughest looking fisherman, stood back to let Cousin La Bott through. It was a little like following Royalty. But she only nodded and walked on to stop beside a car, the like of which Andy had never seen before. It was old, that was one thing, but it looked so frail, so battered, so rusty that Andy thought if he leant on it it would dissolve into nothing. The back bumper, he noticed, was held on by string.

"The Colonel," said Cousin La Bott proudly. The driving door was unlocked, the window was wide open and her handbag for all to see was on the front seat. "He's called the Colonel, because he used to belong to a friend of mine, Colonel Brierley, and when he died I couldn't bear to think of his car being pushed over the cliff. So I asked Chauval to smarten it up and see to any engine trouble. Now he goes very well."

Andy stared at her incredulously. He had never before in his life, not even in Kenya, seen such an old wreck. It – he – wouldn't have lasted on the English roads for ten seconds. He piled the luggage into the boot, taking care to avoid the back bumper and, for once, his feet obeyed him.

"Who? Who is Chauval?" he asked as he sat down beside her in the front, while Kate crept into the back. He wouldn't have been surprised if Chauval turned out to be a gnome, anything seemed possible in this wonderfully strange place. He noticed with some anxiety that there was quite a large hole in the floor and that as they moved off he could see the road skimming along below him.

Cousin La Bott, although dwarfed by the Colonel – she was sitting on a blown-up cushion and her tiny feet only just reached the pedals – drove quite fast smack in the middle of the road. It was very lucky there was so little traffic.

"Chauval works for me on the farm and on the camping site in the summer. We have been friends for all our lives and we have seen . . . But never mind that. You'll meet him soon."

Kate had brightened slightly at the word "farm". That could mean horses or ponies. She and her father had been several times to Kingswood farm and she had always enjoyed seeing the animals and the well-kept stables and exercise yard. They were driving quite fast along the deserted coast road, through a group of low whitewashed cottages which were set on either side. One of them had, painted on its wall, "Eas and emonade". The road divided again, they took the left fork and there was the sparkling sea, but between it and the car there was quite a large area of rough looking grass, a huddle of very old looking buildings, a pond and a very shabby two storey house. To Kate's dismay the car stopped in front of it.

"Welcome to La Bott Farm." Their cousin spoke the words proudly, but even Andy came down from cloud nine as he looked at the building. He'd never stayed anywhere like this before. A small man with bowed legs and a balding brown head came out of the outhouse and waved.

"Chauval," said Cousin La Bott. "Now bring your luggage indoors."

Ten minutes later Kate tiptoed across the landing and into Andy's room where he was gazing out of the window at the sparkling sea. A very large turkey came into view, spreading its magnificent tail feathers at a rough-haired pony, which took no notice as it ambled on towards the pond where some white geese were cackling at each other, standing themselves upright and unfurling their wings as they hurled insults.

"I *hate* it," said Kate and burst into tears.

"Well, how are they Louie?" asked Chauval, padding across the kitchen in his socks and getting down some mugs. The big black kettle was coming to the boil. Cousin La Bott shook her head.

"The boy is big and slow. He may be all right. But the girl . . ." Her hands flew up sideways. "All she does is sulk. No, no that is not quite right. But she's difficult and something is worrying her. I should imagine that perhaps both of them are a little spoiled. These days young people have everything they want."

"Times change." He put his hand on her shoulder for a moment and looked at the grassy bank which ran the length of the little bay. The spring grass was growing fast now, but even so he could still see – all the way along – the blind eyes that were the openings in the now almost overgrown concrete pill boxes. And beyond that, to the left, the grey concrete reinforcements which blended in so well with the rocks that people rarely noticed them now. But they were everywhere still. He sighed and then smiled, his wrinkled sunburnt face becoming much younger.

"Times change and we change with them. Just as well, eh? It'll be all right. Kettle's boiling, I'll give 'em a call. Young ones are always hungry, eh?"

He was right. Andy's appetite, which had never been small, seemed to expand instantly and even Kate managed a few mouthfuls for their cousin was an excellent cook. She even baked her own bread which Andy decided actually came ahead of the chippy as a wonderful smell. But the atmosphere in the small farmhouse was still rather uneasy. Cousin La Bott was obviously not a great talker and Andy and Kate were both shy. They had never been in a house like this before with its enormously thick walls and small windows and all the floors slightly on the slant so that the furniture stood at odd angles. It was left to Chauval to do the talking as he dunked his bread into the stew.

"I remember your father well. Who could forget him, eh? Do you remember when he plucked the turkey feathers and tried to make himself a Red Indian headdress? Or when he rode the pony all the way into town and it bolted with him across the graveyard and . . ."

18

Chauval dried up as he became aware that Cousin La Bott was looking at him with gimlet eyes while Kate and Andy were open mouthed. Could this really be their rather solemn father they were hearing about?

"Dad said that he, er, was sort of quiet when he stayed here," said Andy, suddenly remembering what his father had really said about their cousin.

"Oh he was," Chauval said cheerfully, mopping up the rest of his stew with bread, "Looked as if butter wouldn't melt in his mouth, but underneath he was a holy terror. And it's no good you looking at me like that, Lou. I've seen him across your knee many a time when you caught him out at something. Like climbing over . . ." He stopped.

"Climbing over what?" asked Andy, following Chauval's example with the bread so enthusiastically that he looked in danger of taking the pattern off the plate.

"Oh, oh buildings and things," Chauval gave a wink which only Andy could see. "Shall I get the pudding out of the fridge, Lou? I've got to start clearing the ground for the vegetables to go in."

He was a small human dynamo and after they had somewhat awkwardly helped Cousin La Bott with the drying up – no washing-up machine here, and the fridge and the stove both looked as if they were the same age as their owner – they wandered out into the spring sunshine to where Chauval was forking through the ground. He spat on his hands and rested for a moment.

"Perhaps I shouldn't tell tales out of school," he said, not looking as if he minded in the least. "It was a long time ago when your dad was here and we were all a lot younger then. I remember when I was about your age, Kate, I did some terrible things. It was when . . ." He came to another of his sudden stops and then went on. "Now off you go. You look as though you need some fresh air, go and have a look at the sea, climb a few rocks. There's plenty of bird life out there."

Andy nodded and moved off, with Kate trailing behind him. It was odd to think that only a few days ago she had always been the one who led the way and did the bossing about.

"Come on, I'll give you a hand up this bank," Andy said, but Kate shook her head and leant against the grass. She didn't want to go any further. All she was interested in was getting away from this place as soon as possible. She closed her eyes trying to think of a plan while Andy said:

"OK. Suit yourself."

He scrambled up, taking in great breaths of fresh air and narrowing his eyes against the sunlight. The tide was almost fully in so there was only a strip of sand visible, covered in birds with great long curving beaks which they were using as prods. Those nearest him skittered away but the others went on with the serious business of looking for food. A small fishing boat buffeted its way across the choppy sea beyond the dark rocks, where three large birds, looking remarkably like vultures, were brooding.

All kinds of odd things had been washed up by the tide: a large boot, half a lobster pot, the back of a plastic chair which looked horribly like a collection of bones and great wreaths of seaweed. But what really interested Andy was the fact that the grass bank which he'd just climbed was basically man-made. He pulled away some clods of earth and underneath it was a stone-faced wall with a dark, glassless window.

But why should anybody build what looked like a long row of stone huts and then cover them with grass?

Andy moved on down the beach, the oystercatchers politely getting out of his way rather as the fisherman had done for Cousin La Bott. He could see now that the great arm of rock over to the left of the beach was partly man-made too. But you wouldn't have noticed it if you'd just glanced at it. Curiosity drew him, his feet leaving large prints in the coarse sand. It was the remains of a fortress of some kind. Here and there the concrete had given way and fallen in or been worn away by the sea. The walls that were left were amazingly thick and the windows were far bigger on the inner side of the building than they were on the outside. They narrowed down like tunnels. And there were rusted iron posts everywhere and even some old strands of barbed wire. At the furthest end of the rock and concrete platform there was a great metal circular rail let into the floor. But what it could be for, he couldn't imagine.

The whole place echoed to the sound of the sea which was now at high tide. Andy thought that some time he might try and scramble up and over the roof, guessing that the building went on and through the rock, perhaps even round and over to the next bay which, he reckoned, was the long beach with the harbour just beyond it.

"Andy, Andy . . ." The voice reached him thinly. He shook himself and turned round. A small skinny figure was waving to him from the top of the bank. Reluctantly he started tramping back. Kate looked pale and cold although the sun was warm now. She had her anorak on and she was holding her arms round herself. She began at once in a cross, nagging voice to tell him how they had all been looking for him, and where had he been. She went on and on as they made their way back across the thick soggy grass which was speckled with golden celandines. The rough-haired grey pony came across and stood, shook his head and then ambled over and blew noisily through his nose.

"Oh do shut up," Andy said, not to the pony, but to Kate. "You've been whingeing on ever since we got on the boat. I know it's not like Kingswood, but it's not all that bad. I quite like it, there's a lot to explore. There are all those huts placed along the shore and there's an enormous sort of fortification down by the rocks . . ."

"Shut up."

"What? What's the matter with you?"

"I hate it. I hate it. I HATE IT!"

"Why? Steady up, Kate-o. We can go fishing and water skiing and exploring round all these old buildings and Cousin La Bott's a great cook. I like it!"

Andy let out a great sigh of relief. He not only liked it, he felt at home here. He didn't know anything about fishing or seabirds or even fish come to that. He only knew that his feet didn't fall over each other here and he could spend an hour climbing in and out of rocks and buildings and enjoy it. It was as if he had known this small island all his life.

"Well I don't," Kate said. "I *hate* it. I hate it all. I wish I'd never come here and I'm going to get away as soon as I can. I'm going to ring Mum in Mexico."

"Hi hi hi," Chauval was running towards them from the farm building. "Andy you're a good tall boy, can you give me a hand in the barn, eh? Your Cousin Lou has got it into her head that perhaps we should have extra battening in the roof in case it rains and the weather forecast isn't so grand. That roof's dripped ever since I was a boy and nobody worried. Here, Katy, you OK, eh?"

"Yes," Kate could hardly get the word out. They were right up against the rickety stable block now. She said yes, but she had never felt more terrible in her life. She couldn't breathe properly. It was a lovely warm spring evening, but she felt cold right down to her bones. And she felt so terribly sad.

"Nobody's looked after this building properly for far too long," Chauval said. "Here, Andy, give me a leg up. The last time I was here it was . . ." And he stopped in his usual odd way. "The battens will be over there. Mind your head."

The floor was very uneven and there was hardly any light on the top beams of the barn. Chauval went ahead, muttering to himself, while Andy was trying not to fall over his feet and Kate, as pale as milk, trailed along behind them. She felt as if she were gasping for breath.

"Here we are," Chauval called out. "Yes, I recall when I was about your age, Kate's age, there were battens kept up here, but we never needed them. Give us a hand, Andy. Myself I don't believe these forecasts, there won't be any storm. We're set fair for calm. You take that end, eh? You're tall, you can manage. I'll just be off to feed the pigs."

"Got it," said Andy, several breathless minutes later, and then at last his foot slipped, his arms went round and round and there was no way he could stop himself falling backwards. He shouted, "KATE."

But Kate couldn't move a hand or a foot. It was as if she was tied to an invisible stake. Caught in the beams of light which filtered through the doorway,

Kate could see a shadow of a young man in uniform standing in the corner of the barn, looking at them. She opened her mouth to cry out, and as she did so something quite lightly skimmed her forehead and a voice called out "Heine". After that there was nothing at all.

Val's Story – 1942

Chapter 3

The Wooden Gun

Although it was getting on for dusk, Val could see perfectly well, in fact he had got so used to the blackout when not a light showed anywhere that the other boys called him "Cat's Eyes". It took a minute or two, of course, but then he could begin to pick out the big gun down at the far end of the bay. The first time that had been fired he and his mother had thought they'd been hit by a thunderstorm bolt. Everything in the house had rattled and they were sure the roof had been lifted clean off the rafters. They had thrown themselves on the kitchen floor under the table and Missy, the cat, had gone missing for three days.

But it was only the soldiers firing the big gun. Val had seen it in action a few times now, with its great grey barrel pointing out to sea as it was swung round on its circular rails with the soldiers working like mad men. And what a flash it made, even in daylight. So if you weren't made deaf by it, you went blind. And it drove the seabirds distracted and some of them had left the island for ever. There wasn't a puffin to be seen now. A great raft of them had been sighted, so it was said, setting out from near the Gannet Rocks, but where they had gone to nobody knew. Or indeed if they would ever come back.

Val could tell the time without a watch or a clock and he reckoned he had just on an hour and a half before his mother got back from work at Louie Tostevin's farm so that she wouldn't be caught by the curfew. The soldiers were very strict about that, anybody found out of doors after curfew time was marched down to the old bank which they had turned into a gaol. Even the doctor, cycling off to see to somebody ill or having a baby, had to be taken in for questioning, even if they did let him go ten minutes later. The soldiers did everything by the rules and that was that.

Val let himself out of the house. Nobody about, not a chink of light anywhere, even the cat had vanished into the dusk. Still just in case somebody might be looking Val jerked out his left wrist and pulled back his shabby cuff. He had drawn a watch in ink on his wrist and it looked quite real in the half light. The neighbours would be impressed if they thought he had a watch, especially Dickon. Dickon was almost grown up and fretting to go to sea to be a fisherman like his father. He'd even boasted to Val that once he did manage to get on board a boat he was going to outwit the patrols and get clear away to England. Val took that with a pennyworth of salt because everybody knew that Dickon had been a big talker ever since he was Val's age and his father had sailed him across to the mainland. When he got back he had told the tallest stories in the world about there being cars and motor bicycles everywhere and that in a shop called Wool Something you could buy a real watch for sixpence.

Val grinned to himself in the gathering gloom. There had been other stories too about shop counters in this Wool place where you could buy mounds of sweets. The girls scooped them up in little shovels and weighed them out for you. Val's stomach contracted at the thought. Just sometimes a small piece of bitter chocolate might come his way, but oddly enough it wasn't the sweets of his small childhood that he missed the most, it was *cheese*. Oh how he longed for cheese. He would have swapped everything he had – which wasn't much – for a great big chunk of cheese. Val almost groaned. He tightened the piece of cord which held up his shorts and moved on. Perhaps today his mother might bring back a small wedge from the Tostevin smallholding if the soldiers hadn't been too thorough in their search. Fat chance, they were *always* thorough!

But that wasn't important now, what was, was getting to Dickon's to see IT. Dickon might be a boaster, but there was no doubt that he was good at making things and there was just one of his things which Val really , *really* wanted so much it hurt. And Dickon had promised, and they had shaken hands on it. The bargain was that if Val found him some wire then Dickon would let Val have IT.

It had been one of those amazing strokes of luck and Val's not-too-clean hand gripped the precious cargo in his jacket pocket tightly. His mother had sent him across the street to see if there was an egg to spare from the Ollivers' chickens. And while he had been standing on their doorstep not thinking of anything very much, one of the soldiers had come roaring, well spluttering up the road, in a sidecar motor cycle. Right hand side of the road, of course, not like island people who used the left hand or the middle. And it had spluttered to a stop just short of Val. The soldier climbed off, his long greatcoat and the gun strapped across his back not exactly making life easy for him. He stamped his boots on the cobbles, muttering under his breath and then he caught sight of Val.

"Guten tag," he said.

"Ohé," said Val. It didn't mean anything, it was just a special word which he and the other boys had made up. It drove the adults mad, which was largely the point of it.

"You hold for me?" the soldier said, pointing to the bike. Val nodded his head. It wouldn't do any harm. Perhaps when the soldier wasn't looking Val might be able to loosen the petrol cap so that the petrol would splash out and be wasted.

"Danke." The soldier smiled at him. With his helmet so low over his eyes and ears, it wasn't easy to see much of his face. It was a very ordinary one anyway, a bit like Dickon's with blue eyes and a flatish nose. They could have been brothers. Val went over to him and watched as the soldier began tinkering with the bike. It was a big, heavy thing, so Val wasn't really needed at all, but perhaps the soldier just wanted someone to talk to as he muttered away. Val stood, as he quite often did, with not a lot going on in his head. He was always too busy planning the future. And then his gaze just happened to fall on the sidecar and all the breath went out of him. There it was on the seat – a coil of wire.

Slowly, slowly, Val edged round. Normally he sprang at things, but this was too important. Mrs

Olliver's mother was coming up the cobbles now, she was almost square like a little block of wood and she had her plaited shopping basket over her arm. As she came up to them she turned and said something Val didn't catch and then quite deliberately she spat in the gutter. It was a beautiful spit which at other times Val would have deeply admired, but this was not the moment.

The soldier spun round and half raised his hand while the old woman looked up at him with no expression at all on her wrinkled face. She could have been a wooden figure. But Val didn't notice any of it, his skinny hand shot out and the wire was in his pocket and he was back to his original place holding the handlebars and gazing vacantly into space before the soldier shrugged, muttered something and went back to his engine. Old Madame Olliver grunted and produced the big heavy key to the front door, jerking her head at Val. She said something in a thick patois which he could just about follow and he bolted into the house after her. She shut the door just as they heard the rumble of the motorbike start up. Val was up and running down the narrow passage to the back kitchen just in case the soldier discovered his loss. The wire seemed to be burning a hole in his pocket. But the roar grew less and less and then vanished.

"An egg I suppose it is, eh?" The old woman cuffed him round the ear and then handed him one from the crock hidden under a great iron bucket. "You are not growing fast enough. You had better make it two, eh? I will settle with your mother tomorrow."

It had been as simple as that. Val thought he had seen the same soldier again later in the street, but he had carefully avoided looking at him, so he hadn't been aware of the sad look on the soldier's face, or the way he had sighed and reached for his passbook in its heavy leather folder and looked at the photograph in it.

Val walked on through the gathering dusk. There were no lights anywhere and the island was so quiet he could hear the surge of the sea in and out. Four rabbits skittered across his path and he wished he had his caterpault. Rabbits were getting scarce on the island and his mother's rabbit stew was famous.

Val heard the rumble of his stomach and, for a moment, he wondered what it was like to feel really full of food. But it was too difficult to imagine. He heard the rustle in the bushes, knew at once that it wasn't a rabbit or a rat, and froze into the shadows. It was one of the prisoner people from the camp in that strange uniform. He was the thinnest person Val had ever seen and, one moment, he was there on the dusky track and, the next, he had vanished into the lengthening shadows. Voices shouted in the distance and dogs barked. Val didn't want to get mixed up in anything like that and took to his heels. A minute later he was inside Dickon's front door.

"Are you mad, you? Funny in the head?" Dickon said. He looked over his shoulder at the clock in the parlour. "It's nearly curfew and there's a prisoner got away. Didn't you hear the dogs barking? Well, what is it?"

Val felt his chest swell with pride as he reached into his pocket and produced the wire. He held it up and Dickon looked at it as if he couldn't believe his eyes. Then he pulled Val into the parlour and examined the wire under the oil lamp as it plopped up and down.

"Where did you get this? It's from the soldiers, isn't it?"

Val shrugged and put on his silly face as Dickon examined the wire inch by inch. Then he turned and looked at Val who by now had a face that was so innocent it could have been carved in stone and hung up in the church.

"There's no trouble with it, is there, eh?"

Val shook his head and then studied his feet. There was no hurrying Dickon, but a bargain *was* a bargain! Dickon was stroking the wire as if it were a kitten and then he measured it out, holding his hands wide apart and, with his bright blue eyes and flat nose, he looked quite like a soldier.

"Just about enough," he said. "That should do it. And if and when I get called to go and fish . . ." he winked heavily, "and I get to the mainland, eh, you shall have . . ." he lowered his voice to a whisper, "the Whisker."

Val wasn't too certain what a "Whisker" was or what it was for, but he nodded wisely. Then he went on looking at Dickon, who began to laugh.

"Oh all right, all right," he said. "You have held your side of the bargain, I will hold mine. Come on, IT is round the back in the old pigsty. The soldiers aren't very likely to go and examine that. So IT'll smell a bit, eh?"

Val didn't care. He trotted behind Dickon, almost treading on his heels and then the wonderful moment arrived when Dickon dug away some of the swill and brought out something wrapped in heavy sailcloth. Val's eyes were as round as pebbles in the gloom and neither of them were aware of the distant sound of shouting voices and dogs barking. Even the sound of a rifle shot followed by silence didn't disturb them. They had heard it all before and it was nothing to do with them.

"Go on, take it," Dickon said, "but perhaps you'd better put it under the pump, you not having any pigs, eh?"

Val nodded, he couldn't have spoken even if he'd been paid for it. He took the precious bundle over to the pump in the back yard and started to work the handle until the water began to gush out and over the stinking sailcloth. He was working just as hard as the soldiers did with the big gun when they swung it round to follow the grey convoys out at sea.

"Don't drown yourself," Dickon said. "Here, you'd best be off. It's nearly curfew time and you don't want to get taken off and questioned by Them. If they caught you with that, it might be the end of you, Val."

And Dickon drew his finger across his throat and laughed as he pushed Val back into the house and down the narrow passage, Val clasping the sodden bundle so that he could feel the damp right through his jacket and his flannel shirt. Dickon opened the front door cautiously and looked left and right, but it was too early for the evening patrol and there was nobody about, only Missy, sitting patiently on the doorstep two doors up. A single searchlight swept backwards and forwards across the sky and then snapped off. Val's cat's eyes could see a couple of open backed lorries further down the new coast road which the soldiers had built. The lorries had no lights and they were travelling close together towards the town.

With the rising moon, the sea was brighter than the sky as the waves came lapping in near to high water and about the middle of the bay there was quite a big ship riding at anchor. She was just a dark blur, but Val could see her guns even though they were covered in netting. A rabbit bounced past them and into the gorse bushes.

"Best get back," Dickon said again. He didn't feel at home in the night like Val did, unless he was at sea that was, but then that was different. "Where are you going to hide it, young Val?"

"I've got a place," Val smiled to himself in the darkness. It was best these days to tell secrets to no one, not even your best friend. What you didn't know, you couldn't tell. "Thanks, Dickon."

They slapped hands in the time-honoured way of men striking a bargain and then each made for his own home very pleased with their exchange. Val let Missy in and she slid past his ankles and into the kitchen hopefully looking for food, although these days she largely had to fend for herself with mice and rats. Val very carefully put his sodden bundle on to the worn oilcloth on the kitchen table and began to unwrap it.

Down at Louie Tostevin's farm, Val's mother had slipped off her heavy wooden shoes and was arching her toes. It had been a hard day, but then it always was with only old men and boys, women and girls to do the work. Most of the able-bodied men had been taken away and shipped over to France to work the fields there, but a few had managed to get away in their fishing boats to the English mainland. Val's father had not been so lucky and where he was now she had no idea. There was no use in worrying about it, you had to get on as best you could.

Old Louie came into the kitchen and nodded at her. He was bent right over from carrying heavy sacks over his shoulders all his life so that he looked much older than he really was. He seemed about a hundred by the light of the oil lamp and his face was seamed and wrinkled, but there was still plenty of life in his small eyes.

"Off you go home, girl," he said.

"Oh, Mr Louie, I have to sit, me, just a little."

"There's some tea left from midday . . ."

He put the sack down on the flagstones and moved the big black kettle on to the hob where it began to sing almost immediately. When it was puffing steam he poured a little on to the dried tea leaves. What came out of the pot was pale yellow once the milk and a tiny amount of sugar were added. But Val's mother sipped it appreciatively. Like everybody else she too had got used to tea leaves which were boiled up over and over again. Old Louie helped himself and sat down on the other side of the hob, slurping his tea out of a chipped saucer.

"And how is your daughter?" Val's mother asked, politely.

"She'll do, she'll do. As long as she doesn't answer back to Them once too often." His brow became even more furrowed with creases and wrinkles, crisscrossing each other. "You know what she's like. Answer back to the Devil himself, her. Cooking for Them!" he added in disgust and opened up the front of the stove to spit into it. Then his face brightened and he added, "Still, it isn't all bad. For a good Chapel-going girl she has a light-fingered way. Flour, margarine, an egg or two. Sometimes we gets a couple of Their sausages or a bit of meat. Which brings me to mind that I snared a couple of rabbits. Here, you can have one. Your Val wants to get more meat on him."

Once Val's mother might have muttered politely, "No really I couldn't." But not any longer. She almost snatched the still-warm rabbit away from Old

34

Louie and wrapped it up in her sacking apron.

"Thanks. He's small, but he'll grow," she said and put on her wooden shoes, finishing the rest of her tea.

"You're skinny as sixpence yourself, you," Old Louie said. "You need someone to fend for you, girl."

"Val does that. He's a good boy, on the whole!"

Because of the moonlight she could see clearly up the new road the soldiers had built and she walked quickly, her wooden shoes drumming a tattoo on the tarmac. Not so long ago it had just been a dirt path, wide enough for two carts to pass when fully laden. Then it had been all dust in summer and a bog in the wet months. This was certainly better but it seemed to slope all wrong somehow. And it was later than she thought. If she didn't look out she'd get stopped by a patrol and if they found the rabbit . . . She shivered and walked faster.

Only one more corner to go and there was the little huddle of dark cottages. A small shadow slipped past, it was Missy going hunting. Old Louie was quite right, she did need somebody to fend for her, but there it was . . .

"Oh!" Her hand went to her throat as her heart banged nervously. She *had* left it too late. There was somebody with a gun marching up and down in front of her door. She felt her legs go weak and all kinds of disjointed thoughts rushed through her mind in a jumble. If she was taken away, who would keep a home for Val? The Ollivers perhaps? Old Louie . . .? But surely that was rather a *small* soldier? Only about her own height and then, as he stopped, stamped, swung round and began to march towards her she almost dropped the rabbit in relief.

"Val, Val, what do you think you're doing? And

where did you get that gun? Oh Lord protect us, if They catch you with that . . ."

"But I only . . ."

Gripping the rabbit and apron in one hand, the other descended like a vice on Val's ear as she pulled and pushed him into the house, slammed the front door and bolted it behind them. She was so nervous she could hardly light the lamp.

"Now then, my lad." She put her hands on her hips, taking in great breaths of air. "WHERE DID YOU GET THAT GUN!"

Val laid it down on the oilcloth. It gleamed in the soft light and Val, rubbing his ear tenderly, gazed at it, his face one enormous smile.

"I got it in a swap, me," he said. "I got it to protect you and the house. Nobody could ever tell it wasn't real unless they got really close to it, could they?"

His mother's jaw dropped open. Very slowly she moved to the table and bent down and looked down and then up at Val.

"It's my gun," he said, his voice bursting with pride. "It's my wooden gun!"

Chapter 4

Cat's Whisker

Val could hardly bear to be parted from his gun although his mother told him over and over again that he must never, never, *never* show it outside in the street again.

"It must be hidden," she said. "Yes, yes, I agree that you have been very clever, you, but times are difficult now. Take the bucket and go and work for Mr Louie. But first, hide the – er – gun."

Val could hardly bear to let IT out of his sight. He had longed for IT, wanted IT for months, well weeks, ever since Dickon had showed it to him. But he knew his mother was right and that the soldiers would take it, and perhaps even him, away and maybe he would vanish as people did from time to time on the island, although where they went was a mystery. So every night Val found a new hiding place for the wooden gun but not before, when his mother was at work, he had marched up and down their little bit of cobbled street to protect their house. Somehow when he had the gun over his shoulder he felt like a real soldier himself, an island soldier.

It was while Val was off at work for Mr Louie that he met the German soldier again. Like all loyal islanders, Val had learnt to walk on the left hand side of the new roads because, if they did that, it upset the soldiers in their trucks and motorcycle sidecars as both parties would meet head on. Just before curfew quite a lot of islanders would step out for a stroll and a chat, the women arm in arm and up to four of them in a group. All chattering and with their heads together so that as they came round a corner and happened to meet the trudging prisoners and their guards it was all confusion. Sometimes a potato or some other vegetable or fruit would be passed to the prisoners without the soldiers knowing. Sometimes there was hardly anything to spare at all except half an apple or a pear, a bit of fish or crab, the end of a rabbit or some mussels. But all was snatched away, even a handful of nettles.

Val, for once almost full, most of it rabbit stew which was supposed to last three days, was walking down the middle of the new road with the bucket slung over his shoulder and his mind on the wooden gun when there was an almost familiar roaring noise and a motorbike and sidecar came round a bend in the road. Val wasn't going to move. It was *his* island and he'd been born here. He stood his ground and the bike came to a stop. The rider and Val looked at each other. Val's stomach dropped about two inches. It was the soldier who had been carrying the wire. He knew who had stolen it and he had come to arrest Val and take him away. Val straightened his shoulders and waited as the soldier, once again, got off his machine somewhat hindered by his long grey coat and the rifle across his back.

Slowly he advanced towards Val, who somehow managed to stand, small, skinny and determined in the middle of the road.

"Guten tag," the soldier said and actually held out his hand in a big leather gauntlet. Val stared at it and then up at the soldier. He hadn't the least idea what was going to happen next. The soldier cleared his throat.

"You are 'das kind' the boy who hold the bike for me? Ja?"

Val said nothing. That was something he had learnt: when in trouble say nothing at all. He remembered the last place he had hidden the wooden gun, yes, that was safe enough, and then gazed stolidly up at the soldier who was reaching inside his jacket. He took out a heavy-looking leather wallet, opened it up and flicked through until at last he reached a photograph. He took it out and held it towards a very bewildered Val.

"Is my wife," said the soldier. "Now we have a son. A baby like you."

Val looked up, deeply affronted. He had got over his fear about the wire he'd stolen, but what all this photograph and baby stuff was about he hadn't the least idea. And the last person who had called him a baby had got a very bashed nose.

"No, no," the soldier smiled faintly. "My English is not good. One day my son be large son like you."

That was better. Politely, Val took another look at the photograph. He felt quite sorry for the soldier if that plain person was his wife, with her hair all wound up round her ears and a silly smile on her face. She wasn't a patch on his own mother who, for a middle-aged person of thirty-three could be quite pretty sometimes. But he still didn't know what it was all about.

"I have not seen my son," the soldier said, carefully putting the photograph away. "He is born since I am here. One day . . ." He stopped and looked away and then shook himself. "What have you in the – er – ?" He pointed to the bucket.

Val, still not speaking, held it out with some glee. It was swill for old Louie's pigs and it smelt foul. There were bits of rabbit's fur which even his mother couldn't find a use for, boiled bones, rotting onion skins and the remains of the hunting prey which Missy had brought in. The soldier stepped back hurriedly and then looked at Val again.

"You eat?" he asked incredulously.

Val hunched his shoulders right up to his ears, his bony hands out-stretched sideways as he had seen the French fishermen do. In a *way* they ate it because sometimes old Louie managed to slide them a bit of pork offal after he had killed a pig. He had to be very clever to do it, because all killings were carried out in front of a soldier cook who knew about these things. But then Louie, like his daughter, had learnt how to become very light fingered these days.

The soldier shook his head again and swung himself into the saddle as a whole convoy of motor-cyclists and trucks came round the bend in the road. One of them shouted something at the soldier and, whatever it was, it seemed to make him very angry because his face went red and he shook his fist at them and shouted back. There was a whole series of jeers and catcalls and Val continued to stand stockstill where he was with that blank look on his face which made him appear totally witless. It worked now, because while all the drivers sounded their horns and began to shout at him, he just gazed back and, in the end, they had to detour round him. It wasn't much but it gave him a small feeling of triumph.

He hadn't the least idea what it had all been about and, anyway, he wasn't interested. All he wanted to do was to deliver the evil bucket, do a bit of a scrounge round – as long as there was nobody about – and then get back to the wooden gun. He had been studying the soldiers so he knew how to present arms and how to come to attention and then to stand at ease, stand easy.

There was mist lying out at sea, like a rolled up grey mattress and, once he had delivered the swill and been given half an apple by Old Louie and cuffed round the ear, Val made off down the farm track with the cleaned-out bucket over his shoulder, his hands in his pockets and his cheek bulging with apple which he was chewing over very slowly to make it last. Then he saw Old Louie's daughter coming towards him and stepped smartly into the hedge. She was only ten years older than he was, but she behaved as though she was at least twenty years his senior. She always called him "Boy", which he hated. *And* she was a good inch shorter than he was. But she had a tongue like a rasp and he didn't want to tangle with her. Dickon *said* that he had heard her giving the soldiers what for in the market in town. In patois, of course, but Dickon had heard enough to make him shoot off, just in case the soldiers had realized what she was calling them. But instead they had clapped and whistled. Very strange.

She sailed past him, carrying a bulging plaited bag over her shoulder and resting it on her hip; her tiny wooden shoes going clack, clack, clack on the hard road and then clop, clop, clop on the farm path.

*"L'affair va-t-elle?" she asked in patois as she sailed past.

"Ohé."

To his utter astonishment she stopped, dipped into the bag and pushed something into his pocket. And then she was off again moving, as usual, twice as fast as anybody else on the island. Val felt cautiously at the shape of the tin, made sure there was no one about and, in the safety of the hedge, drew it half out. He didn't understand what was on the label, that was all in the soldiers' language, but he could guess from the picture on it that it was milk. The wonderful sweet thick milk which he had tasted twice before. His mouth watered and he swallowed the rest of the apple, pips, core and all.

This was his lucky time: rabbit stew, an apple, sweet milk. It was wonderful. And the wooden gun. He eyed the mist. Yes, it was going to come in shore with the tide. He could see it moving stealthily towards the gun emplacement and the end tip of the long barrel suddenly vanished. Val squatted down to wait. It didn't take long and then as it swirled in over the concrete pill boxes and the soldiers were swallowed up in it, Val was off like a rabbit and down to the site where the prisoners worked. They had all been herded into their concrete block houses by now, late afternoon, and the sentries had turned in as well. He could hear them over at the far side of the big field, laughing and talking. They had a kind of shop there where they could buy bottles of beer and tobacco and some sort of food. Val had watched them from afar, but, of course, he had never been too near.

He went under the low wire like a ferret down a

*How are things?

hole, leaving the bucket under a bush. With his cat's eyes he could see the lines of mounds and he knew what that was. Potatoes. Dickon had taught him how to go "midnight shopping" as it was now being called on the island. You didn't just snatch at the first thing, that was too obvious and could lead to house-to-house searches of peoples' larders. No, you took one here and one there, and you pushed the earth back again so that it didn't look as if a human hand had touched it. He filled the pockets of his shorts and then his jacket and he was about to wriggle his way backwards when he heard the voices over by the soldiers' shop get louder. They were all shouting and then one voice shouted back and, for a moment, he thought it might be the voice of the soldier who had shown him the stupid photograph. But it was nothing to do with him, all he knew for certain was that it was time he cleared off quick, sharpo.

Val wasn't quite so clever getting back under the wire, as his body shape had swollen a bit with all the potatoes he now had on board and he heard his jacket rip as it caught on the shiny barbed wire. Too late to worry about that. He collected the swill bucket and ran for it up the road, his skinny legs moving fast and his feet in the big boots which had once belonged to his father fairly thudding along. He saw Madame Olliver in the curling mist, but she was too busy searching for firewood to notice him and his mother had gone up to the town market. Mr Jean Olliver, who had been a fisherman, a farmer, a market-stall holder and a soldier, so he *said*, appeared slowly through the mist, nodded at Val and limped across the road and into his house. He limped a lot these days, but that was mostly when the soldiers were about. Certainly nobody could call him able-bodied and he always seemed even older than his own mother. That was another mystery.

Val picked up Missy and put her down on the stone floor then, very carefully and with a great deal of pride, he laid out the tin of milk and the potatoes on the oilcloth. His mother would be proud of him. That was a great deal of food. Val reclaimed the wooden gun from its latest hiding place and began to polish it. He heard a patrol go by. The mist was so thick by now that it had grown quite dark in the kitchen so he took the gun to the back door, cradling it on his lap.

"Hey, pst. Ohé!"

"Val nearly dropped the wooden gun. His heart bumped and then steadied down. He would have recognized that whisper anywhere.

"Ohé," he whispered back and over the wooden fence at the bottom of the plot a familiar shape appeared out of the mist. Dickon came towards him looking very pleased with himself.

"It's good that gun, then, eh?"

"The best."

Val looked up in alarm. Dickon was his friend and they had slapped hands on a bargain so he couldn't want the gun back surely?

"Sit back, Val, you," Dickon said softly. "Come and see what I've made now. It leaves the gun well behind. Hop over, the soldiers are about this evening. There's been some sort of trouble down by the camp. A lot of shouting and that, eh?"

"What have you made now?" Val asked as they vanished like two shadows into the mist. It muffled every sound but, distantly, they could hear voices shouting down towards the prisoners' block. It was that strange time of day when almost all the light has gone, but it isn't near nightfall. When the sea fog rolled in like this it made the sound of the swell grow louder, but you couldn't hear a bird cry anywhere.

Dickon's house was just like Val's, but not quite as clean. Dickon's mother had never been quite the same since her husband vanished on his fishing boat sailing for the mainland. These days she just sat in front of the stove and rocked backwards and forwards in her wooden chair with a shawl over her head and round her shoulders. Dickon was used to it, but somehow the house always made Val feel itchy up and down his back.

"It's out here," Dickon said, taking no notice of his mother, but then she didn't take any notice of him. "In the yard by the pig sty. Just you wait and listen young Val. Oh, one day, I'm going to build a much better one."

"Better what?" Val whispered.

"A wireless; a proper, real one. You wait."

They both stopped whispering as they heard a patrol go by. The shouting down at the site had stopped and a rather blurred searchlight was trying to get through the sea mist without much success. Then the big gun started up so that the sound waves rolled back and made all the windows rattle.

"It's here, see," Dickon took told of Val's thin wrist and pulled him towards the old garden hut where Dickon's father had once kept pigeons, his fishing nets and lobster and crab pots. But they had almost crumbled away by now. A little further on was the railway line, a single track which the soldiers had made as good as new although it was a hundred years old. Once it had been used to bring stone up from the big quarry to build the great Victorian forts which ringed the island but, although since then it had carried a certain amount of stone to keep the breakwater secure, nobody had bothered about it very much. Only now it was in pristine order bringing out even more quarried stone to build the modern defences, the great block houses, the gun emplacements, and the passages which now ran underground like mole tunnels beneath the island. It was said that great crates of ammunition were stored there.

"Here," Dickon said, his eyes lighting up. "I wouldn't tell anyone but you, Val, but I know you'll keep a quiet tongue in your head. Look what I've made. And look where the wires go; right over the railway, across the old telegraph poles. The soldiers'll never notice that, because it looks as if it should be there you see, eh?"

Val had no idea what Dickon was talking about, although he could see the wires, oh my gracious, *his* wire, his stolen wire, snaking over the poles just as Dickon had said. And the near end of the wire went into the chicken hut.

"What's in there?" Val asked, hardly recognizing his own voice.

"Come and see, young Cat's Eyes."

Val would far rather not have done so. He'd had quite enough excitement for one afternoon what with thinking that he'd been caught for the stolen wire and then going *under* the wire. But, of course, he couldn't lose face in front of Dickon or he'd never hear the last of it. Reluctantly, he followed the older boy into the hen house. It smelt to high heaven, so that it caught in his throat and the big rooster came out of the gloom, its crested head jerking backwards and forwards. The three hens crouched in the far corner until one of them stepped forward, put her foot in the water dish and upset it.

"No brains, them," Dickon said, pushing his hand under the matted straw in the rickety nesting box. He brought out the strangest object, or collection of objects, that Val had ever seen in his thirteen years: two small roundish black things rather like flat half eggs; a lot of twisted and coiled wire, more flat shapes and what looked like a very small piece of coke. It didn't any of it make any sense to him and he wasn't sure he liked it much. He put on his stolid face, but his eyes had noticed that one of the wires vanished through a hole in the wall of the hen house.

Val wasn't stupid and he realized that must be the wire which went snaking over the railway line. But why? What for? Dickon was crouching down, his eyes shining in the gloom. He pushed the rooster aside and said in a whisper, "When I went to England that time. My dad, he bought me this book which tells you how to make things. Remember that churn I made for my mother? That was in the book too."

Val nodded silently. Who could ever forget that churn and how it had sent the goats' milk flying all over the yard and how Dickon's father had howled with rage and chased after his son with a stick.

"I was only young then, eh?" Dickon said, looking back across the gulf of three years. "But I'd have got it right in the end if my father hadn't chopped it up and used it for stove wood." And he sighed at the injustice of life. "One day I'm going to make all kinds of things. I'll be an inventor and live in England, you'll see."

"Mmmm," agreed Val. It was cold as well as smelly in the hen house and he wanted to get home to see his mother's face when she saw the potatoes and the milk. "But what does it, that little wire thing, *do*?"

"It's called a Cat's Whisker . . ."

"Not Missy's . . ."

"No, of course not! Shut up and listen. The whisker's a piece of wire. You put on these head-phones, like this . . ." He slid them over Val's ears and then pulled them forward slightly as he went on in a breathy whisper, "and then you move the wire over the crystal like this . . ."

"But what does it do . . .?" Val began again. There were strange noises in his ears, noises which he had never heard before in his life; scratches and then sorts of bangs and plops. Val's short hair quite literally went up on end. It was far more frightening than going under the prisoner's wire. It was ghostlike and, for a moment, he remembered the blood curdling stories about "Le Sorciere", the island spirits, which his grandma used to tell him at night when he was small.

Val was about to snatch off the headphones when, through his ears, came the sound of a sharp peep, peep, peep noise followed by a man's voice: "Here is the News and this is Frank Phillips reading it. On the Russian Front . . ."

Val was still gaping as the headphones were snatched off his head and thrust under the chickens' straw. Half a second later Dickon's large hand was over his mouth. They ducked down, not breathing, as through the thin wood walls they heard the sound of a patrol stamping over the cobbles.

Chapter 5

The Warning

How long the boys crouched there they had no idea and even the chickens seemed to have gone quiet. There was a second patrol coming along the railway line but they weren't marching and, because the mist had made the runners slippery, there was the sound of boots hitting the pebbles between the sleepers. That was all bad enough, but it was the dogs they were listening for, the big dark Alsatians which pulled at their leads and whined and growled at the backs of their throats. They wouldn't be fooled by silence, they could pick up the scent of a frightened person from yards away.

But their luck was in, there were no dogs tonight. Perhaps they had been left behind to restore order at the camp after the trouble down there. Voices called to each other over the low housetops as the two patrols on parallel lines moved on and slowly, slowly were lost in the mist.

The two boys let out their breath and Val discovered

that, far from being cold, he was drenched in sweat. He said in a very hoarse whisper. "They nearly heard us, you!"

"Not us, the BBC. That is the Wireless Station in England. It's hundreds of miles away."

"Then how do we hear it here, on the island?"

"Oh, that's the way it works. But it means that we can know what is going on away from here. We shall be told when the soldiers are beaten and they will have to leave us free here and I can look for my father."

Dickon spoke fiercely, in a way which Val had never heard before and, for a moment, his world seemed to grow larger and to expand far beyond the island, the only place he had ever known.

"I must go home," he said. He'd had enough for one day and he wanted to be back in his familiar kitchen, but as they crept out of the hen house, he whispered, "You must be careful. If you were caught with that Whisker, it would be very bad for you, eh?" There had been one *real* wireless on the island – big thing in a sort of box. It had belonged to the post master, but both he and it had vanished long ago.

"Me, I won't get caught," Dickon stretched himself in the deep gloom. He was a good head taller than Val and he went on, "but it's good though, eh?"

"Very good."

They slapped their hands together and then Val slid away soundlessly.

His mother was waiting anxiously at the front door. She cuffed him quite hard round the ears, but he knew that was only worry.

"Where have you been, eh?"

The locks and chains rattled across the door and

Missy went flying up the narrow passage with her tail in the air. "What do you think I feel?" his mother's scolding voice went on. "All that food on the table – where did you get that tin? – and you nowhere to be seen and then two patrols coming past. Supposing they had come in here? What would I have said? How could I explain? Come on, come on where did you get that tin? You never stole that? Val you don't understand. To you it's all a game, but it's *dangerous*."

Val let her rattle on. In a strange way it was comforting to hear that scolding tone and to know that she was only *worried* about him, not really *angry*. And here in the little kitchen with the thick curtains over the windows and the lamp plopping up and down he felt safe.

"Oh, you!" His mother suddenly ran out of breath as he knew she would, and she gave him a small push, rubbing the edge of her apron across her eyes with a faint smile. But she stuck to her point as she made Val sit down and then stood over him with her hands on her hips.

"Where did you get that tin?"

"Old Louie's daughter gave it to me!"

"What! Her? That stuck up one?"

Val nodded and grinned.

"Yes, her. She's not so bad. When can we open it? Now? This evening?"

"Old Louie's daughter! Well! *And* you've torn your jacket. You went into the prisoners' quarters didn't you? Oh, Val, Val. Well it's all done. Yes, we'll open the milk tonight."

And she sat down suddenly as if all the strength had gone out of her. It crossed Val's mind for an instant that he could tell her about the Whisker but she would probably go quite mad. The really important thing was that they were going to have another good meal: boiled potatoes and tinned milk. Nobody could ask for anything more than that! Everything else was forgotten.

By silent mutual consent Val and Dickon kept away from each other for a couple of days. They both knew it had been a close thing with the Whisker, but Dickon was so proud of his achievement that he had to show off to someone. His mother was no good, she didn't even know the time of day any more and there were no young people in this part of the island unless you counted Old Louie's daughter, and she was always off early in the morning to work in the town and back late in the evening. And anyway she rarely spoke to anyone as her father had land and was, therefore, an important person.

Dickon stuck it out for two days, as did Val. Dickon was busy putting out spider crab pots down by the breakwater. The soldiers allowed that, although they walked up and down all the time with their guns under their arms, watching him. Val joined him with his father's boots tied by their laces and slung round his neck. His mother liked him to wear the boots, but Val preferred to have his own bare tough feet under him when he was walking on something as slippery as the breakwater.

They stood side by side and looked out over the churning grey water to where the soldiers' ship had gone down in a storm not long ago. As it was slack water they could see the prow sticking out. There was a small soldiers' boat fussing round it and an important looking man giving a lot of orders.

"Caught anything?" Val asked.

His mother had mended his jacket with twine

which smelt salty and he had jammed his cloth cap down on his head, back to front.

"Not much," Dickon said. And then, out of the corner of his mouth, "It said last night on the Whisker that there's bad fighting for the soldiers in Russia."

Val kept a respectful silence. He hadn't the haziest idea where or what Russia was, so he changed tack.

"So it's working all right then, eh?"

"It's very good, eh? Listen Val. I'll tell you this because you are my friend. One day I shall sail off. When that happens I may not have time to tell you, me. So you look after the Whisker and my mother."

Dickon turned and looked at Val. Somehow it seemed as if his blue eyes were looking far away at another world.

"There's a pot needs coming up," Val said. It was as if a great weight was coming down on his shoulders. How could he help his own mother, hide the Whisker and see that Dickon's mother was taken care of? He just wanted to go shrimping or carrying the pig bucket or kicking a football. At thirteen it was young to have to become a man.

"You're right, there is a pot needs coming up," Dickon said. "Give us a hand, ohé."

Val was crouched in the hen house, the ear phones clamped over his ears, listening to words he hardly understood when the patrol, moving very quietly for once, came to Dickon's front door. Dickon was in the kitchen giving his mother some soup. He had only left the Whisker for two minutes when they knocked. He had five seconds in which to make up his mind and he did it all in that time. He opened the back door and reached up and pulled down the wire so that Val suddenly heard himself listening to nothing except a thudding kick on the hen house door. Then Dickon opened the front door.

The soldiers were very orderly and polite. There were three of them and Dickon thought he recognized, in a hazy sort of way, the one who was in charge. He was sure in his own mind that they had come for his Whisker but, like all islanders, he had learnt that silence was the best thing so he just stood, looking bewildered.

"I will go out to the back," the first soldier said. "Every person stand as you are."

Dickon's mother hadn't even moved, but then she was in her own world.

The soldier walked down the dark garden to the hen house where Val, with his heart thumping somewhere under his chin was fluffing up the straw and throwing round the grain he'd picked up from the ground. The rooster was following him and feathering up his wings. Val knew the soldier at once. He was the one with the wallet and the photograph. Val squatted back on his heels so that he was almost sitting on the Whisker.

"Listen," the soldier said, in a low voice, "you are 'das kind'. A child, a boy. One day my son will be a boy like you. I have seen the aerial of the wireless, you understand?"

Val nodded. He wasn't frightened any more, it was as if everything was starting to slide past him, faster and faster, and he couldn't stop it.

"The wireless must be 'kaput'. You must stop it or *you* will go *and* your mother. You understand?" He drew his hand across his throat and at the same moment Val heard Dickon shout out, "no, no, no".

When they got back to the kitchen there was no one there, then there was a sound of a truck moving off.

The soldier, his gun under his arm, whispered, "Kaput! You understand?"

Val nodded. He didn't understand at all what was happening or where Dickon and his mother had gone or why, but he went back to the hen house and picked up all the wires and the earphones and jumped up and down on them over and over again until they were nothing but small pieces and powder. Then he let the rooster and the three hens out of their smelly house so at least they could be free for a while.

It was as if Dickon and his mother had vanished off the face of the earth, but then news began to filter through as it always did on the island. Old Louie's daughter picked up the first rumour in the town where the soldiers called her "little cat" because she snarled and hissed at them, like a kitten with its back arched. But they had got used to her and were sometimes careless in what they said. She had a good ear for languages and was rapidly picking up their foreign words and she was fluent in patois and English. So, as her small hands kneaded dough and rolled bread, her ears were laid back. And what she heard she reported to her father.

"It is said," she told him, using the old island formula when one was not too sure of one's facts so that if you *had* got them wrong they couldn't be told in court against you, "it is said that Dickon has been sent to Normandy to work in the fields."

"Oh, eh. He is big enough now, him. I would have liked him here on my fields. Why was it done?"

His daughter spread her hands. "Because he is a big lad? There was some trouble at his cottage. They were looking for something, but what it was I don't know. They didn't seem to find it. Perhaps he had extra food?"

Her father's creased face became even more wrinkled, all the lines going down so that he looked like an old dog. He had the big milk pails on the kitchen table and he was turning them slowly. Somehow the milk didn't smell as sweet as it should do. Perhaps it had something to do with the rats? He had never in all his life seen so many rats on the island. Or as many rabbits, he thought, brightening up slightly.

"And the mother?" he asked.

"Oh, she has gone to Cachaliere. You know for those ones who are . . . ." and she put one finger to her head.

"I know, I know," he said grumpily. It was a house which had been built over a hundred years ago as an isolation hospital for troops building the great forts and the breakwater. It was a warren of small rooms, one leading off from the other. He had been inside it once when he was delivering milk and he had got quite lost.

"It will be better for her there. She will be looked after and fed properly. Dickon is big, but he is still young and he didn't really understand what had happened to his mother's mind."

There was a short pause while they both went on working. The camp site was quiet tonight and the mist of the night before had given way, as it so often did, to a clear night full of stars. When Old Louie's daughter went to the back door to take out the pig swill she could hear clearly to the far side of the camp. The soldiers were singing tonight, some kind of rather sad song as though they were homesick. Her father's gruff voice brought her back into the kitchen.

"And what about the hens, eh?"

"What hens?"

56

"Are you out of your wits, too?" He hit the heavy table with the flat of his powerful hand. "Dickon's hens? Who will look after them?"

His daughter half smiled, but said nothing. She knew which way her father's mind worked. But, as he was to find out, for once he had been out-thought.

Val's mother came in early in the morning to begin her working day at the farm and as she tied on her sacking apron, she said, "So, is it true that Dickon's gone to Normandy?"

"So it is said."

"Eh, eh, eh." She began to pile up the heavy wooden furniture so that she could sweep and then scrub the stone floor. She did it every day, and every day it was dirty again.

"And the mother?"

"Cachaliere."

"Well, she will be near the new hospital the soldiers have built. It is only across the road. A stone's throw . . ."

"I must go," Old Louie said, heaving himself to his feet. "It has just come to me. Someone must feed those poor hens of Dickon's."

"No need," Val's mother kept on sweeping without missing a beat. "Val is looking after them. You know how he and Dickon are such firm friends, eh? When Dickon gets back Val will have everything all straight for him."

It was Val, still on edge about there being any remains of the Whisker, who had thought of the chickens first. He had hidden all the bits of wire in the swill, which, even now the pigs were eating out in their pen at the back of Old Louie's house. It didn't seem to bother them at all. And it was while he was sifting through and through the hen house that he realized properly that Dickon was gone. Perhaps for years, perhaps for ever.

Val rocked backwards and forwards in a way which his mother did sometimes when she was tired. Then the cockerel came in from the patch at the back of the cottage and looked at him, beadily.

"Food," Val said. He knew where it was kept, in the sacks in the outhouse. The hens and the rooster went for it greedily. He filled up their tin water bowl and one of them, as usual, trod in it. Some things in life never seemed to change much. Val sighed, pushed up his chin and went to get the wooden gun from its latest hiding place. It made him feel better to have it lying across his knees as he polished it with an old rag. He would keep it until Dickon came back. How quiet the cottage seemed now as he locked up with the heavy key. He was about to put it into his pocket when he heard a voice from the shadows.

"Hey hsist . . ."

For one glorious moment he thought that, by a miracle, Dickon had escaped and come back home again. Whoever was flattened against the wall was about the right height. Then, with his cat's eyes, Val saw the glint of a gun barrel and the shape of the helmet and his heart began to beat very quickly. He straightened his knees and gently shifted the wooden gun behind his back.

"It is all right," the voice said softly. "Das kind. I am alone. You also?"

For a wild moment, Val thought of saying that there were three enormous fishermen in the kitchen, but he knew it was no good so he just nodded his head. They looked at each other and, for the first time, Val spoke to the soldier. He owed him, eh?

"Thanks."

58

The word came out gruffly and the soldier nodded his head.

"It is kaput?"

It was Val's turn to nod. He might not be able to talk other languages like Old Louie's daughter, but the Whisker was very definitely kaput, he knew what that meant all right. In fact at this very moment the wire which he had taken from this soldier was now inside the pigs' stomachs.

There was an awkward pause and then the soldier said awkwardly, "I come inside? A moment only."

Although he had his stupid face on, a great deal went through Val's head very quickly. The tin of milk was hidden under a brick in the outside larder. The potatoes were in a sack, and anyway who could tell one potato from another? And the rabbit was all gone. But there was still the question of the wooden gun. But then the soldier had a *real* one. Val edged back trying to find his own key, hang on to the wooden gun and not damage the two warm eggs in his jacket pocket. It was quite difficult, but luck was on his side because old Mrs Olliver, who didn't understand what a curfew was, came stumping at that moment down the road in her wooden shoes. The soldier melted back into the shadows. Val had the door open and himself inside in one breath, and the wooden gun under the table. In spite of his heavy boots the soldier moved very quietly. Val closed the door behind him.

He had no idea what was going to happen next or why the soldier wanted to be there. Val's mother would be home soon. It was her night for a late pass, getting the milk ready to be collected, but she wouldn't like a soldier in the house. She always looked sideways with her head down when the patrols went past. Was the soldier going to ask him

59

questions? About the wire for the Whisker? About Dickon?

Val stood rigidly with his arms to his side in the middle of the kitchen while the lamplight plopped up and down and the soldier, his rifle half off his shoulder, walked slowly round and round. He was searching all right, checking on the shelves, opening the cupboard doors, even taking the grid off the stove. Val watched him silently, slowly moving round on his heels as the soldier examined everything. He could see the wooden gun under the table out of the corner of his eye.

"It is like my house," the soldier said, "my kitchen also. You have enough food?"

Proudly, Val took the two speckled eggs out of his pocket and put them on the table. They were his and nobody could take them away from him. Well they could, of course, because the soldier's gun was a real one, but somehow Val didn't think that would happen. There was another silence and then, surprisingly, the soldier turned back to the cupboard where Val's schoolbooks were stored along with his rulers, paints and pencils. There hadn't been any school for quite a long time, ever since the teacher had been taken away to work in Normandy. Val hadn't really missed him a great deal.

"You let me have this?" the soldier said. And he put the paintbox that Val's mother had bought for him two years ago as a Christmas present on to the kitchen table. "And I give you this . . ." And out of a pocket the soldier produced half a loaf of greyish looking bread and a hunk of yellow cheese.

It didn't take Val more than half a second to make up his mind. Who cared about an old painting box when faced with cheese? He almost held out his hand to slap hand to hand on a bargain. But that was only for islanders, so he nodded his head instead and then, in the distance, they both heard the clicking of wooden shoes.

"Guten nacht," the soldier said and bowed his head. For a moment he did look very like Dickon and not much older, then he was gone. Val looked at the cheese and the bread and wondered how he was going to explain it all to his mother as she came hurrying up the road followed by the whistling and shouting from the camp site.

Val began to eat very fast to get rid of the evidence. But *why* did the soldier want Val's paints? It was another mystery. Missy came stalking in and Val fed her a piece of cheese. It was very strong and different from their usual rather mild cheese. Val's mother's footsteps were coming round the corner of the street.

"Ohé," Val said to Missy, who had just unfurled herself from under the stove. Val wished very much that Dickon was with him to explain everything. But Dickon was gone, as so many had gone, perhaps for ever. Val rubbed his hand across his nose, pushed the wooden gun even further into the shadows and went to open the door for his mother.

Chapter 6

The Painting

Val crouched like an old man down on the harbour wall. He had Dickon's spider-crab pots now because nobody else had claimed them. Dickon's mother in the Cachaliere didn't know if it was Monday or Friday, or so it was said. And there was no word of Dickon in Normandy.

"So Val," his mother said, "we might as well have the crab pots and the hens, eh? Better us than the soldiers?" And she spat in much the same way as Old Mrs Olliver did. Val's spirits went down a bit and then the thought of his gun cheered him up. Whatever happened he would hang on to that.

"Ohé," a voice said in his ears and Val nearly dropped his pot line. The soldiers were bringing up their wrecked ship in bits and pieces and the important looking officer was worth watching. He talked and shouted, waving his arms about so much it was surprising he didn't fall into the sea. Val had been so interested that he hadn't noticed anybody else.

He turned round and there was Old Louie's daughter, as small and neat as ever with her arms crossed under her shawl and her big straw bag over her shoulder.

"I'm from the market, me," she said in her usual brisk way. "So where is Eric La Bott?"

"Haven't seen him," said Val who, as usual, was hollow with hunger.

"You find him quick sharp for me and there'll be a milk tin and some cheese and sausage – what is that then, eh?"

Everybody ducked, soldiers, fishermen and those working on the raising of the wreck, as a plane streaked overhead. It flew so low it had to put its nose well up to clear the fortifications at the far end of the harbour. It was the fastest thing Val had ever seen in his life, and he stared after it with his mouth wide open.

There was a distant rat-a-tat-tat, which sounded very close in the stillness that had fallen over everybody. Then there was a flurry of movement round the wreck, with the officer shouting louder than ever. A distant burst of gunfire came from the site on the far side of the harbour, but it was obviously far too late to do any damage to the plane which had long since vanished into the blue sky.

"It was from the mainland," the girl said in a whisper from behind her small hand. "Go on then, Val, shut your mouth and find Eric La Bott. You know I can't go looking for him, me."

It was understood that girls and women never went into the dark little bars which ringed the harbour and the town, but boys, from their very earliest years, were allowed to do so. Warmed by the thought of endless tinned milk, cheese and sausage, Val wormed his way into the nearest bar. But there were only a few soldiers there and Old Louie's cousin, Ed Tostevin, behind the bar who jerked his head at Val to clear off round the back. Ed was a big, serious looking man, who had lost part of his left foot in a fishing accident when his boot had got caught in an anchor rope. As it turned out it had been a blessing in disguise for him, otherwise he would have been sent off to work on a farm in France. As it was, he kept his face serious, but he listened to everything the soldiers said. The beer smell in the air was thin and sharp and all the soldiers were crowded round the window, which was criss-crossed with tape, as they talked about the path the plane had taken.

"Wait a while, and I'll give you a job," Ed said, "but you're too small and skinny now. How old are you then? Ten?"

"Thirteen!" Val said firing up, his short hair bristling.

"All right, all right. Your mother is well?"

Val nodded and turned his cap between his fingers. Then he remembered Old Louie's daughter waiting for him outside and he said, "Where is Eric La Bott?"

"At sea," Ed said sharply, "Who wants to know?"

Val ducked his head to the narrow doorway and, past the kegs and barrels, they could both see the small, upright figure waiting impatiently. Ed chuckled and said quietly, "So that is how it is. You can tell her he'll be back the next Ormer tide. He's too useful to the soldiers bringing in the lobster and the fish for them to send him off. He brings me a little too. Here's something for your mother. And for you. You look as if you could do with it."

Val watched as Ed moved back into the darkness of the cellar, counting out the barrels until he came to one which he knocked gently with his knuckles and, as Val's cat's eyes got used to the gloom, he saw Ed slide the cask sideways and take out the wooden end. Inside was a smaller one attached to the tap, so that if anyone turned it on beer would come out. But packed into the space that was left were beautiful silvery fish. It smelt wonderful as Ed wrapped it in some dirty paper and pushed it into the bag which Val had hoped to fill with spider crabs. But this was much better.

"Off you go and do some growing, eh?" Ed said, laughing. "And my good wishes to your mother. One day I'll come and visit, me."

Val politely shook Ed's hand and then said rather belligerently, "Dickon?"

Ed shook his head. "If I hear I tell you." He turned on his heel and went back into the bar where the soldiers were now thumping their beer mugs on the counter and asking for more. Old Louie's daughter took the news of Eric La Bott's whereabouts quietly and then fell into step beside Val.

"You going to marry him, then, eh?" Val asked.

"Mind your business."

Her small hand flew round his ears, making them ring, but the colour came up into her face and she began to walk faster than ever so that Val, although he was an inch taller, had to run to keep up with her on the uneven cobbles. They had to dodge to get out of the way of a lorry crowded with soldiers and then a whole stream of motorcycles with sidecars. They reminded Val of the soldier he had begun to know a little. If there should be more food coming from him how would he explain it to his mother? The answer was at his side.

"There's some food I *may* get, not much. I have to tell my mother something. Can I say it's you?"

The girl came to a stop, her hands on her hips as she looked at him squarely in the eye. Val gazed back, at his dullest. But she wasn't fooled for an instant.

"Are you under the wire, you? At the camp site?" Val shrugged.

"You be careful. If they catch you there you are gone . . ." And she drew her hand across her throat. Val continued to look at her without blinking. She put her head on one side and then started walking again. "It's not my business," she said under her breath. "The less we know of each other the better it is. All right you can tell your mother it is me, but if, if, you are caught, I shall say I know nothing. You understand?"

Val nodded. You didn't slap hands on bargains with a girl so a nod would have to do. They walked on back along the new curving road by the bay, hardly seeing the line of prisoners who were shuffling along on the far side as they went to work on the new harbour wall. It was best not to see such things. As they reached Val's home she slid her hand into the plaited bag and, half a second later, two tins were rattling in Val's pocket. He ducked his head, waited until she was a safe distance away and then said, "Good luck with Eric La Bott!" He was pleased to see the back of her neck go crimson.

It was a week later, when the fish was but a blessed memory, that the soldier turned up again. Val hadn't been back to the camp site, his mother had strictly forbidden him to do so. She could hear the sound of shouts and shots from Old Louie's farm and you didn't need to be too clever to realize that there was a lot of trouble there. So Val had taken his caterpault down from behind the back door and gone off looking for rabbits. There were plenty of them about, more than ever before in living memory so it was said, but the difficulty was that they would go springing off into the fields where the soldiers had put mines. The rabbits were too light to disturb them, but Val had once seen what had happened to a cow which, in a fit of madness, had leapt the barbed-wire fence. Not even bits of it had been found.

There were times when he wished desperately that the wooden gun was a real one so that he could have gone out at night and – with his cat's eyes – shot one of the many rabbits. He missed Dickon all the time, like a heavy weight inside him. So, when the soldier did come round about an hour before curfew, Val was almost glad to see him. The soldier seemed to know exactly when Val's mother would be out. Perhaps he watched her movements at the farm from the camp site. Tonight he looked awful. His eyes were bloodshot and one side of his face was swollen and discoloured and, when he smiled, Val saw that a tooth was missing. He came in quietly and once again he went round touching things, stroking the wood of the sideboard, lifting up the old black kettle and then sitting down slowly in the wooden chair as though it was the most comfortable seat in the world.

"Well, mein Kind?" he said.

Val ducked his head, his eyes on the soldier's rucksack and the piece of wrapped-up wooden board he was holding under one arm. The soldier smiled faintly, put the rucksack on the table and gestured to Val to open it. There was a tin of sausages, some more of the greyish bread and a hunk of the strong smelling cheese. Val looked at it, swallowed noisily and then looked at the soldier, who nodded. The food was off the table and out of the back door in one movement. It was getting too dark for anybody outside to see where they were hidden and anyway these days with Dickon and his mother gone, there wasn't anybody *to* see.

"And now," the soldier said and began to undo the sacking which was tied with thick string round the board. Before he took it away, as though he wanted to make the moment last as long as possible, he took Val's battered old tin of paints out of his pocket and laid them on the table. Val watched in silence. He couldn't for the life of him think what on earth was going to happen next. The sacking fell to the stone floor, the soldier took a deep breath and turned the board round to face Val.

It was a painting of a soldier and a woman. She was carrying a baby and all three of them had very round eyes and were looking straight out of the picture. Val was no artist himself but even he could tell that this was not a very good picture. In fact it could have been done by a small child, but there was something about it, about those painted eyes staring and staring. It made him think of Dickon, and Dickon's mother silently nodding to herself in the old isolation hospital, and the silent shuffling prisoners who he always tried not to see. And the sounds they heard sometimes down at the camp site and, suddenly, for the first time since he could remember, he didn't feel hungry because his stomach was held in tight.

"That is me," the soldier said quietly. "Und my wife und meine Kind. I wish that you would see it."

"Er," said Val. He remembered a lone word he had learnt, 'Er *gut*.'"

Was that right? He was out of his depth. These days he was always finding himself in places where he didn't know what to do and, without thinking, he reached under the stove and brought out the wooden gun. Even as it came, gleaming and perfect into the yellow light, he knew he had made a mistake. The soldier got to his feet in one quick movement, staring down the barrel of the gun. His eyes were very blue and because of the shadows his nose looked more squashed than usual. In spite of the grey uniform and the bruised side of his face, he could almost have been Dickon. Only Dickon would have laughed softly and said, "Ohé. Who are you frightening now, eh?" or something like that. The soldier only let out a great breath of relief and then sat down again, blowing out his cheeks. His face was now the colour of Old Louie's milk. He reached out his hand and took hold of the wooden gun. He turned it over and over and stroked the barrel, shaking his head.

"It is good. But it must go," he said quietly. "If you are found with this, do you know what will happen?"

Val nodded. It was always the same story. If you had tins on you, or extra food of any sort; if you made a Whisker; if you were out after curfew; if you had a wooden gun; if you trapped a rabbit; if you went under the wire and dug for potatoes; if if if; if you dared to breathe too much air . . . it was always the same answer. You would vanish.

And then Missy came stalking in from the back larder with her tail up and a ferocious grin on her face. Between her jaws was the most enormous dead rat. Very slowly and carefully she dropped it in front of Val and it lay there, with its four paws held up and its long tail stretched across the stone floor.

"The cat eats well," the soldier said and laughed. He and Val looked at each other and it was like being with a friend. Slowly the soldier got to his feet, doing up his tunic and looking round for his gun and then after one last look he put the sacking round the picture again and tied up the string. He bent forward, clicking his heels together.

"Things are not good at the camp," he said, touching his swollen cheek. "I do not like what happens there. Es ist nicht gut. And when I say that I get . . ." and he grinned and touched his cheek again. "But the – er – gun it too must be kaput, mein Kind."

"Ohé," Val agreed, because it was easy to say and really didn't mean anything. The soldier left as silently as he had come, slipping away into the darkness. It was a clear night again and Val sniffed at the air. Spring would be coming soon. He could hear the sound of his mother's footsteps coming up past the camp site and away from Old Louie's farm. And then one of the low searchlights blazed out and there were voices shouting. The tap, tap, tap of his mother's wooden shoes grew louder and suddenly from across the cobbled street Val heard Old Madame Olliver hiss, "Get in, boy, get in and shut the door, you. This is not for us."

Val obeyed without even thinking about it and half a moment later his mother joined him. After she had slipped the chains and locks over the front door, she bent over taking deep breaths.

"Oh there is trouble there, eh? Old Louie is in a state, him. Something about his daughter being courted by that Eric La Bott. Well we shall see what we shall see. And the prisoners and the soldiers are fighting and then there was this aeroplane which flew here. It is said it is from the mainland. Can they fly so far as this? I am sorry there is no supper tonight except soup again . . . Val, what is this?"

Slowly and carefully Val laid out the food that the soldier had brought him. His mother's eyes grew as round as the eyes of the soldier's wife in the painting. She looked at Val with her anxious face, her hands gripping her old shawl. "Where did you get all this?"

Val looked at Missy who was just finishing the remains of the rat under the stove.

"From Old Louie's daughter, her," he said and the colour didn't even come into his face. Long ago when he was young he had been told not to tell lies, but now it was the simple thing to do to protect his mother . . .

They looked at each other and then she glanced away, saying, "Well, it's food, eh? And you're not the only lucky one. Look what I caught on the wire!" And she produced what looked like half a grey sweater, dirty and oil covered. "You wait till you see what I can do with that. Have you fed the chickens? Mr Louie says he can let us have more grain for them, but he says too that the milk smells bad. He is sending it to the camp for the soldiers . . ."

She was talking a lot more than usual this evening and Val knew that she was nervous about something, but after they had had their evening meal she quietened down as she began to undo the piece of knitting stitch by stitch.

It was at times like this that Val missed Dickon most and even the Whisker. It had been very interesting in a muddled kind of way hearing about some of the things which were going on away from the island. Like looking through a sea mist.

"Val," she was looking at him intently, "promise me one thing. Don't go under the prisoners' wire. There are bad things happening at the camp. Old Louie has heard and so have I . . ." She stopped and bit her lip. "And Old Louie's daughter, she understands some of the things the soldiers are shouting. There is trouble between themselves. They are

71

fighting down there and tonight one of those big tanks came round from the lighthouse road . . ."

Her voice trailed away and both of them remembered the time when the soldiers had first arrived and the islanders had gazed with their mouths open at these enormous, heavy, noisy machines as they rumbled over the cobbles. In fact some of the town roads had grown great holes because the tanks were too heavy for them and the sewer pipes had broken.

"It came round from the lighthouse road and it is now at the camp gates, almost opposite Mr Louie's farm. He is not at all pleased. He is afraid that if that gun goes off so will his roof." And she gave a shaky laugh.

For one chilly moment, Val wondered what his mother would say if she knew that less than two hours ago one of the soldiers had been sitting here in the kitchen giving him food and showing his painting. Val glanced sideways, he could see the faint shadow of the wooden gun under the stove. And then Missy broke the silence by edging herself forward, so full of rat that she could hardly move. Val and his mother both laughed and Missy pushed herself round so that she had her back to them. She began to purr in a deep, rasping rumble.

But long after he was in bed, wrapped in the coarse grey blanket which tickled his nose and the back of his shorn neck, Val could still see in the darkness the picture which the soldier had painted. And he knew now what the soldier had been thinking about: about being home and warm and safe. Val drifted into a deep sleep. He didn't even hear the sound of gunfire down by the camp site.

Chapter 7

The Hunt

It was Val who saw the soldier first this time when he was halfway down the railway line, hiding in the bushes with his caterpault at the ready as he stalked a grey rabbit. Old Mrs Olliver, wheezing and complaining and spitting as magnificently as ever, had gone trudging into town, while her son, his lame leg apparently very bad this morning, was sitting outside his front door on an upturned pail pretending to mend some ancient fishing nets. Val knew very well that it was pretending because Mr Olliver had never been known to do a real job in his whole life. Old Louie's daughter had gone clacking off up the hill road to the town with her plaited bag over her shoulder as usual and Val's mother had gone clacking off in the opposite direction to the farm. So now it was all quiet.

There were hardly any birds about. The sky was pale blue and there was a long, large grey ship carrying big guns, coming round the end of the breakwater. There had been some talk about the aeroplane which had flown so low yesterday, but now even the camp was quiet and the prisoners had long since left on one of their silent, shuffling marches to the harbour. Great new stone buildings were going up everywhere along the southern cliffs and, it was said, there were passages and tunnels not only under the town now, but coming almost as far as this end of the railway line and the cottages. Although what they were for nobody knew, something was certainly being stored in there because a small railway had been built and the loaded trucks went rattling off into the tunnels quite regularly.

The soldier was on foot today and, like Mr Olliver, he was limping a bit, only in his case his face showed that walking really *did* hurt him. There was something odd about him and then Val realized that he didn't have his gun strapped across his back. The soldier stopped in front of Mr Olliver, who made a great show of getting up slowly and clutching at his back. But then he just stood and shook his head and grunted, and Val knew that the soldier was asking where *he* was. For half a mackerel he would have stayed where he was, safely hidden by the bushes, but somehow he just couldn't leave the soldier to go off again, looking worried. And indeed today he looked worse than ever, with his face almost as grey as his uniform.

So Val slithered out from his hiding place, ducked across the line and then over the back wall and round the side of the cottages.

"Hist," he said, just as the soldier had said to him. The soldier turned sharply and came across. Mr Olliver watched him, his small eyes full of curiosity and then obviously decided that it was better not to interfere. With no sign of a limp he was up and inside

74

with the net and the bucket and his back door was shut.

"Mein Kind, I have to talk with you."

There was another bruise on the soldier's face and he caught his breath as he sat down in the kitchen. Val put the old kettle on the stove and sorted out the best of the dried tea leaves while the soldier watched him, his hands dangling on his knees as if he were an old man. He took a deep breath and gazed at the pale, hot drink which Val handed him silently. It was almost now as if they were old friends. They hardly needed to speak. The soldier blew on the pale tea, waving away the offer of milk.

"I am now going away," he said.

Val looked at him enquiringly, his head on one side.

"I am in trouble." The soldier smiled faintly and then rubbed his bruised face. "I do not like what happens at the camp. I say so. It is not good. So I am leaving. It is said perhaps that I go to Russia."

Val stared at him, remembering the bits and pieces he had heard on the Whisker and the man who had spoken from The News, wherever or whatever that was. The things he had said about the Russian Front had not been good at all. There had been a great deal of fighting there with a lot of soldiers on both sides being killed.

It was a warm and sunny day outside, but in the kitchen it seemed suddenly to get very cold. Missy came out of a deep sleep, leapt out of the window and vanished.

The soldier and Val looked at each other and Val knew quite certainly at that moment that he would never see him again. It was as if once again he was saying goodbye to a friend. And this time he didn't even know his name.

"And I must also tell you, mein Kind, that tomorrow there is a big search. All will be looked at. *All*, you understand?"

Val nodded, a great lump of misery coming up in his throat. He looked down at the stone floor with his hands behind his back and a ferocious expression on his face, his hair bristling more than usual. The soldier got up, came over to him and put his hand on Val's shoulder.

"That is the way it goes," he said, "for you. For me. One day perhaps it all changes. But if you are found with the gun – the wooden gun – you know what?"

On heavy feet Val went and got the wooden gun from its latest hiding place. He laid it on the kitchen table. It was the best thing he had ever had in his life. Dickon had made it and when Val held it he could at least pretend that he could defend his home and his mother with it. Of course he knew it was all pretend, but now even that was being taken away.

"Es ist so gut," the soldier said, stroking it. "Aber – but if it is found here – you understand?"

Val scowled at him and the soldier cuffed him round the ears as if he had known him all his life. Then he picked up the gun and slung it across his back as if it really was a real gun. It looked wonderful.

"I also hide the painting," the soldier said. "My painting. Me, my wife, mein Kind. One day it will all be different, but not yet, I think." He clicked his heels together and bowed his head.

Val put out his calloused small hand and the soldier did the same. They smacked hands as if they were friends and had made a bargain.

"Val," Val said.

"Heine," the soldier replied, and a moment later

he was gone. Val picked up his caterpault and returned to the railway line. His wooden gun was gone, gone for ever. He knew that and he lay down on the ground with his arms and legs spread out until the sun went down and it began to get cold. Then he went home.

"Where have you been?" his mother said in her scolding voice. Then she took one look at his face, put her arms round him and rocked him backwards and forwards in the middle of the kitchen. Val didn't hear a lot of what she said. Then she sent him off to feed the chickens and he was halfway through that when he heard the thud, thud of .the motorcycle patrol coming up the road. Everybody else had heard it too, because all the cottages were quiet. So quiet they could hear the ships' engines as a whole convoy came round the harbour wall and into dock.

"We are searching," the soldier's voice seemed very loud. "Please open up the doors."

Val came silently through the back door and he and his mother looked at each other. They straightened their backs and did as they were told. Missy went over the back wall.

"We are searching," the sergeant said again, stepping heavily into the passage.

There were only three of them, but compared to Val and his mother they looked very big and bulky. They didn't seem to like their job and the youngest of the three kept giving Val's mother small, apologetic smiles. But she only stood silently in the middle of the kitchen with her hands clasped in front of her, her gaze firmly fixed on the wall. It was as if the soldiers didn't exist. Val felt scared and angry at the same time. He hated seeing their boots scratching the stone floor and their hands moving pots and pans. They took all the food out of the larder, but there wasn't much and the youngest soldier caught Val's eye for a moment and slightly nodded his head.

Val hadn't the least idea what he meant and he didn't want to know either so he looked away quickly. The sergeant thumped through the two bedrooms, scattering the blankets on the floor and turning over the horsehair mattresses. He even shook the photograph of Val's father so that it rattled in its wooden frame. Val saw his mother stiffen and went over to her, took hold of her wrist and held it tightly. She was shaking a little, but she still didn't speak. The sergeant led the way out of the back door and across the yard. They could hear him scrambling over the wall to Dickon's house. A moment later, there was a furious squawk from the rooster and all the hens began cackling as well. It made Val smile in spite of himself, but he was half afraid that the sergeant might come back with four limp bodies in his hands. He didn't, but he was picking feathers off his uniform, and sucking one finger. Val thanked his lucky stars that all traces of the Whisker had vanished so completely.

"Danke." The sergeant clicked his heels together and bowed stiffly to Val's mother, who continued to look past him at the wall. His face got a little red and he turned and marched off down the narrow passage to the front door with the second soldier almost on his heels. The third soldier, the young one, stepped hurriedly up to Val as he pulled a bulky object out of his uniform pocket.

"For mein Kind, from Heine," he said in a low whisper and was gone as the sergeant started shouting for him. Val's mother fortunately had started tidying up, so she didn't see what had happened and, as the front door slammed shut, she said irritably, "Now what was all that about?"

"I don't know," said Val, although he could guess. Perhaps somebody else had spotted the Whisker or the wooden gun or seen Heine the soldier coming into the house. It was said that sometimes people were paid with food for saying what their neighbours did. It was always better to say nothing. But, having been searched by the soldiers who had found nothing, *he* now had something new to hide from his mother. Val stuffed the neat parcel down the back of the old sofa which had springs coming through the horsehair.

"Pigs, cochon," his mother said, sounding so exactly like old Mrs Olliver that Val half expected her to spit into the stove. "Well at least they didn't find this!" And to Val's utter amazement his quiet, polite little mother hitched up her skirt to disclose a small bundle tied round her leg. Val goggled at her as his mother actually started to giggle.

"Mr Louie gave it to me. He's been butchering one of his pigs. Two chops Val and some suet. Tonight we eat as good as our Duke of Normandy, eh?" And she began to laugh even more loudly. Val joined in and for once it was a relief to have the heavy curtains over the windows. It kept in the wonderful smell of meat cooking.

Val was aching to know what Heine the soldier had sent him and why, but he couldn't own up to it until he'd had a word with Old Louie's daughter. Life was getting very complicated. In the morning, with the smell of the meat still drifting in the air, his mother was her usual calm self again.

"Old Louie says you can come and work for him today, digging the ground. He won't pay money, of course, but it'll be food, perhaps clothes of some sort."

Val didn't much like the idea of inheriting any of Old Louie's clothes as they smelt quite badly but he'd worry about that later.

"Finish clearing up. I've washed the blankets in the copper – but there's no soap left. It will have to do. Hang them on the line. Feed the hens," his mother instructed. "And bank up the stove and shut it down and I will see you at the farm in less than an hour."

"Ohé."

His mother clicked her tongue at him and went hurrying off with her plaited bag, wooden shoes clacking. There was a patrol coming over the hill with some of the shuffling prisoners, but they might have been invisible as far as his mother was concerned. Val turned back indoors. Now at last he could undo the parcel. It was tightly done up in a greasy oilskin which unrolled to disclose a piece of greyish soap, a tin of milk, a tin with a picture of a fish on it, a slab of bread, a piece of the now familiar cheese, some bright yellow margarine, a twist of paper with fresh tea leaves in it, another twist with coarse white sugar and a third piece of paper containing coffee beans. There was also a tin knife, fork and spoon.

Val spread it all out on the shabby sofa and a minute scrap of paper fell out. Neatly written in pencil were the words, "Mein Kind. From Heine."

Val knew what these bits and pieces were, he had seen others like them. It was Heine-the-soldier's rations. They were all he could give to a friend who he would probably never see again. Slowly, Val wrapped them up again, although not as neatly, and put them back in their hiding place. He would have to have another word with Old Louie's daughter. Well she was renowned for her "midnight shopping". Perhaps if he offered her the fish tin they might have a bargain?

Val glanced at the parlour clock. He had a lot to do before he joined his mother. Today he was going to become a real working person with a job that paid in food and clothing. He wasn't just a boy any more, a boy with a caterpault, or a pretend wooden gun. It all went hazily through his mind and then, while he was hanging the heavy grey blankets on the line, he heard the shuffling footsteps of the prisoners going past and for the life of him, although he had been taught over and over again not to have anything to do with that side of island life, Val had to go to the front door.

They were trudging past in their usual way, wearing their bleached uniforms, their faces bearded and their eyes looking straight ahead. There were soldiers on either side, their rifles slung across their backs and then more soldiers behind, marching as briskly as they could at this slow pace, so that their knees came up quite high. And in the middle of a row of soldiers Val saw Heine. He too was looking straight ahead, just as the prisoners did, but as he reached Val's house his eyes looked sideways.

Val could hardly see his face because of the close-fitting helmet but for a moment they were able to glance at each other. Val stopped scowling, half smiled and ducked his bristly head. And then Heine was gone, swept away as Dickon and his mother had been.

Val listened for a moment to the dragging footsteps and the marching boots and then went back to feed the hens and bank up the stove. Otherwise his mother would tell him off from here to Christmas!

Chapter 8

Air Raid

It was getting on for curfew time when Val was at last allowed back into the kitchen by Old Louie. He ached and throbbed in every part of his body. He had no idea you could hurt all over so much and it had only been a digging job he'd had. But then the fork had been nearly as big as he was and every time he had stopped for a deep breath Old Louie had somehow been there with the creases on his face all running downwards like a hunting dog's.

"I don't think too much of this boy of yours, eh?" he had shouted at Val's mother. "Too small. No flesh on his bones. He'll never do."

And then, surprisingly, Old Louie's daughter had come clattering out into the yard with her hands on her hips and had actually answered back to her father!

"Now then, you," she said, "stop being after the boy like that. He's doing a very good job, him."

Everybody stopped work. It was unheard of that a

daughter should answer back to her father before other people and Old Louie was the most surprised of all. His lower jaw went slack, but not for long. He picked up his waistcoat and roared, "Who are you talking to, girl?"

They faced up to each other while Val and his mother stared, open mouthed. They glanced at each other and then back again to the arena. None of them were aware of a far-distant engine noise in the sky.

Down by the harbour the soldiers had arrived and were lining up along the harbour wall with the prisoners. The large grey ship was at anchor and the rest of the convoy was standing off, waiting their turn to come and unload. Most of the wreck had been dismantled and taken away and there was only the boiler sticking up high and dry on the rocks in the middle of the bay. One or two of the soldiers' heads turned slightly as they heard the distant aircraft, but nobody was particularly worried as they had all the guns they needed to protect themselves. And anyway they had never been attacked.

Back at the farm, Old Louie was roaring at his daughter like a wounded bull, only worse.

"When I want you to tell me what to do, I will tell you, me, eh?"

Val just stood there with his head going from side to side. He hadn't really got much idea what it was all about except that Old Louie's daughter seemed to be on his side for some reason. And then, even more amazingly Old Louie fought his way into his waistcoat, turned round and said over his shoulder, "So why are you saying all this about Val? Eh?"

"Because," his daughter said, her chin up and her eyes sparkling, "Val helped me. Look then."

And she held out one grubby little hand on one

finger of which was a ring. It was made of minutely plaited wire and, for one instant, Val had a sudden picture of the wire that Old Louie's pigs had eaten.

"It is from Eric La Bott, fisherman," Louie's daughter said. "We are going to be married."

The sun was going down and the mist was starting to curl in from the sea. Over to the north, the lighthouse was sending out the small flashes of light that were used nowadays. They came through little slits at the top of the tower, not at all like the broad flashing beams the island had once been used to.

"Married." Old Louie sat down heavily and, quite suddenly, he looked a lot older and more creased than before. Val's mother went over to him and Val saw his chance. It was now or never.

"Um, could you say that you, er, found a whole lot of soldier's rations and things and that you – er – let me have them?" Val stopped suddenly and then smiled right across his dirty face. "Well I was the one, eh, who got the message to Eric?"

"Oh you, eh?" she said, admiring her ring. "All right, it's agreed. You tell your mother that. Ohé, what is *that*?"

They all heard it at the same time, the engine noise which had been steadily growing louder and louder. It sounded like the plane they had heard down at the harbour, but now there were a great many of them.

All their worries were forgotten as Old Louie and his daughter, Val and his mother ran out of the farm building. The camp was quiet tonight and there was a big round moon coming up over the misty sea. It was bright enough for all of them to see the tops of the long line of ships waiting to come into the harbour and particularly the big ship which was anchored close in shore.

The roar of the aeroplane engines was worse than the thunder of the tanks. They had a kind of whine to them and they seemed to be getting very close. The beam of the lighthouse had vanished and there was not another light anywhere, only an eerie greyness with the big moon shining down.

"Draw the curtains," Old Louie said hoarsely, "and then under the table, the lot of us. Do as I tell you."

The curtains rattled across on their heavy wooden poles and all four of them met head on under the great table. The whining sounds grew louder and louder then, after a moment's silence which seemed to last for ever, came a series of tremendous bangs, so loud they hurt Val's ears. He covered them with his hands and felt his mother put her arm across his back as they knelt down, their noses almost touching the cold stone floor. Then the guns started up, even the big one so that round the edges of the curtains there were continuous brilliant patches of light.

Boom, boom, boom . . .

Val heard one of the windows crack and the glass tinkle into the kitchen. Nobody said anything, or moved. They were quite helpless; all they could do was wait. Then there was an even more terrible sound, as if a giant sheet of paper was being ripped apart, then the great roar of an explosion and, in spite of the curtains, the kitchen was lit with a fierce red light. Underneath all this Val thought he could hear voices shouting, klaxons sounding and the terrified squealing of the pigs. A second window shattered and the bits of glass sliced through the heavy curtain, fell on the table top and skittered across the stone floor. Saucepans fell clattering from the shelves and there was a separate heavy thud.

It was like being in the middle of an inferno which seemed to last for ever. Then the noise of the planes began to recede and the thud of the engines grew fainter although the guns continued to fire. Pom, pom, pom . . . Rattle, rattle, rattle . . . The sound of the klaxons and sirens increased and so did the shouting. A lorry roared past, taking the corner so sharply they could hear its wheels squealing on the new road. And all the time the broken glass fell tinkling into the kitchen.

"They've gone," Old Louie said. "Mind how you move. There's a lot of glass broken, eh?" And he sighed heavily. He had lost two windows, maybe more upstairs and there was no replacement glass on the island so everything would have to be boarded up. And his curtains cut to ribbons . . .

Then Old Louie, like the other three, forgot his fears and worries. They were still alive and unhurt, that was the important thing. Val had even forgotten his aches and pains, indeed they vanished as all four of them crunched across the glass to look through the tattered curtains. It was as if the whole island was on fire and, although they were a good three quarters of a mile away, they could feel the heat on their pale faces.

They hadn't got a clear view of the harbour because of the great gun emplacement and block house which the soldiers had built at the far end of the bay. But they could see the end of the harbour wall, or what was left of it, and beyond that, out to sea, two of the grey ships were burning like torches. The mist, not grey now but a vivid red, made it all look worse. The block house itself was ringed with the brilliant garish light which meant that something really big must be burning in the middle of the harbour. There was a whole series of explosions and lights flared up into the sky.

Nobody spoke. It was like nothing they had ever experienced before, it was almost too big to understand. Old Louie's daughter thought of Eric and squeezed her eyes tightly shut. But Eric was big and strong and he had survived storms at sea and even a shipwreck out beyond the Casquet Rocks. A man who could do that could survive everything. Val's mother thought briefly of her husband and then stopped, as she had taught herself to do, and laid her hand on Val's bristly head. Old Louie's mind had turned to stampeding pigs and Val wasn't thinking about anything at all. For once his mind really was blank.

Two more lorries went roaring past and the klaxons seemed to come right at the farm and then race away again. Old Louie shook the curtain and more glass tinkled on to the floor.

"They belonged to my grandmere," he said.

"Tomorrow I'll see if they can be mended," Val's mother said, doubtfully. They looked more like plush lace curtains now. "Here, I help you sweep up . . ."

They hardly needed the oil lamp as the kitchen was still lit by the great glare from the inner harbour, but somehow the lamp made it seem safer and more secure. Val's mother brought some wide, wooden clothes pegs out of the kitchen drawer and used them to hold the torn curtain together as best she could. Then she went and got an old horse blanket and fixed that over the rail. It looked odd and it smelt, but it cut out the light from the burning. Val and Old Louie's daughter began to pick up the scattered saucepans and jugs and the glass which seemed to have got into everything and Old Louie himself went off in pursuit of the pigs. When he got back the kitchen looked almost normal and he sat down heavily in his big wooden chair.

"You can stay here tonight if you want to," he said.

Val's mother drew herself upright, her face at last getting back some colour.

"Thank you, but no. I'm a respectable woman, me," she said. "Come, Val."

To everybody's surprise, Old Louie threw back his head and gave a bellow of laughter. Val's mother grew pinker than ever and Old Louie's daughter started to giggle. So did Val. It was like the top coming off a boiling kettle.

"You'd best get off then," the old man said huskily, looking at the stolid black kitchen clock which, although it had been blown flat on its face, was still ticking resolutely. "It's curfew in five minutes, but I doubt if they'll worry about it too much tonight. I'm slaughtering tomorrow. I'll see there's something put aside for you. A Respectable Woman! Hey!"

They could hear his rumbling laugh following them into the red darkness and Val's mother said, "I never slept but in two houses in all my life. My parents' house near town when I was a girl and then in your father's house when we married. And I don't mean to change my ways now. No matter what the aeroplanes and the guns do!"

It was comforting to hear his mother talk like that and they set off briskly for home, although they had to make a quick leap up the bank a couple of times as more lorries hurtled past. They could see grim-faced soldiers crushed into the back, swaying backwards and forwards as the lorries skidded round the corners. Because of the lie of the land, the harbour and whatever was happening down there was hidden from their house. But the sinister glow was still in the sky and the explosions were continuing, although they were partly cloaked by the mist.

Missy, apparently undisturbed, was asleep in front of the stove and all their windows were intact, although a couple of saucepans had fallen off the shelf and the photograph of Val's mother and father on their wedding day was very crooked on the wall. Val watched his mother go to pump up some water and got Heine's rations out from the back of the sofa. His mother was very distracted still and took the story that it was a present from Old Louie's daughter without a blink.

"Best not to mention it much, eh?" Val said.

"I know that, you stupid boy," and she cuffed him round the ears, which was a sure sign that things were back to normal.

Val thought that with all that had happened and being scared nearly out of his head he would have nightmares, but not at all. The moment he was under his grey blanket he was gone. It could have been the supper of tinned sausages and the potatoes or the tea with tinned milk which very nearly filled his stomach that did it. Or working all day at Old Louie's farm and the promise of more food tomorrow. But he fell into a deep pit of sleep and not even the continuing explosions disturbed his dreams. His mother came into the doorway and looked at him, sighed, and then went back to the kitchen and picked up the rough wooden knitting needles and began to rock backwards and forwards as the needles clicked. The unpicked and washed grey wool was to make Val a proper wool cap like the fishermen wore. Missy watched her with gleaming green eyes in the firelight.

★

It was a beautiful morning and there was even a single bird singing somewhere. The previous night might have been a dream itself if it hadn't been for the smell of burning and the powdering of ash and dust everywhere. Each bush, each blade of grass, the road, the roofs, the hen house, all were covered in it and the windows looked as if they had been boarded over.

"Give them a wash down," Val's mother said, briskly. She looked heavy-eyed and pale, but in her manner she was quite her old self. She had decided to ignore the air raid and the fires, just as she took no notice of the soldiers or the prisoners. She gave Val his usual string of orders and then, much to his surprise, squeezed his shoulder before she went clacking off down the road, calling over her shoulder, "And don't be late for work, you."

"Working now are you, eh?" said Mr Olliver, limping out from his house. He looked up and down the road, but there wasn't a patrol in sight so he just walked normally to his front doorstep and sat down on it.

"Ohé," agreed Val, moving at double speed as he pumped up water into the heavy iron bucket and then, with a sliver of the soldier's soap, began to clean the windows.

"I'd work if I could, of course," agreed Mr Olliver, "but it's the wound in my leg, you know, eh?" And he patted it affectionately. "That was a rumpus all right last night. Bombing us! Where will it all finish up, that's what I ask myself, me. Would you like to help out by doing these windows as well . . .?"

But Val had already vanished back into the house and had washed up, banked down the boiler, vaulted the fence to get two eggs, fed the hens and the rooster, shaken out his blankets and was off while Mr Olliver was still talking about how he hadn't managed to get a wink of sleep.

"The young haven't got any respect these days," he grumbled, watching Val running off down the road towards the harbour. Val worked it out as he ran. He'd done everything his mother had told him to do in about fifteen minutes. It would take him another ten to run to the harbour, so that was twenty gone, and from the harbour to Mr Louie's farm twenty five minutes, and he'd have to sprint a bit, so when he got to the harbour all he'd have would be ten minutes. He had to know what had happened last night and if Heine-the-soldier had been on the big grey ship and where it was now.

But as he came round the corner, Val could see all too clearly what had happened. It was a sickening sight. A great pall of smoke and dust still hung over the inner harbour and there was wreckage everywhere, which, taken by the tide, had been swirled in and now littered the beach and had even been swept up to the criss-cross of barbed wire which ringed the seashore. The wreck of the boiler out on the rocks had a string of other wreckage around it and there were blackened skeletons of boats out to sea. Val took off his father's boots and tied them round his neck by their laces. He ran on barefoot. He just had to know *everything*.

He reached the harbour which was full of soldiers, most of them also covered in ash and dust. The lorries were lined up and so was row after row of still forms under dusty grey blankets. They were being carried, one after another, to the trucks and lifted on board. Right alongside the damaged harbour wall was all that remained of the big grey ship: just mangled pieces of iron in all kinds of odd shapes which stuck out from the oily and filthy sea. They were like great grey bones. Val had once seen the remains of a whale which had been washed up on the island and it made him think of that, except that this skeleton still glowed with heat so that every time a small wave came rolling in and touched it above water level it hissed venomously.

Val stared at it all and suddenly he wished very much that he was young again, when food and the wooden gun, his mother and Missy and moonlighting potatoes and perhaps a rabbit were all that mattered. But when he looked at the boots sticking out from under the grey blankets and the few dented, scorched helmets stacked in a pile and he knew quite certainly that somewhere here was the soldier. Somewhere in this line after line of blankets and boots. And that the wooden gun and the painting too were gone for ever.

"Val!"

A heavy hand fell on his shoulder and he nearly jumped right out of his skin. It was Ed Tostevin, Old Louie's cousin. His face was all black with smoke, his eyes were red, and he'd got ash and dust on his hair, what there was of it.

"Your mother is all right, her?"

Val nodded, still fighting for breath. His heart was going like a rabbit's.

"And cousin Louie and his daughter?"

Again Val nodded. Ed Tostevin cuffed him lightly round the ear and took a deep breath.

"You can take a message, you. Eric La Bott is fine. He was fishing for the soldiers out beyond Casquet Rocks. Had a good haul too. Some, I daresay, may come your way, if you're a good lad?"

"I'm working for Mr Louie now, me," Val said, squaring his shoulders. He looked away from the grey blankets and the twisted, mangled wrecks of the ships and up at Ed Tostevin.

"Is that it, then?"

Ed nodded and neither of them took any notice of the soldiers marching down the harbour wall, nor of the lorries starting up and the activity amongst the fleet of small boats – under the direction of the officer who always shouted such a lot. It was as if they, the soldiers, didn't even belong on the island any more.

"There's always a job for you here, Val," Ed Tostevin said. "Remember the message."

He put out his hand and he and Val smacked them. It was Val's first grown-up bargain. He had got a job and after that another job, and a message to deliver and one day he would tell somebody about Heine. Without knowing quite why he did it, he took off his cap and put it on the nearest blanketed body. It was all he had to give.

But now he had to run as fast as he ever had in his whole life and, with his skinny little elbows going like pistons, his father's boots clattering round his neck, his baggy shorts flapping and his eyes set straight ahead, Val set off down the harbour, along the harbour road and then to Old Louie's farm. He didn't know what he was running away from, but only that he had to go faster and faster until he was back with his family and friends and they were all together where they belonged.

Chapter 9

Chauval

Kate lay quite still, her face the colour of milk, with one arm across the wooden batten which had skimmed across her forehead. There was a slight red graze over one eye and she looked as if she had just fallen asleep in the patch of sunlight which was streaming in through the long-ago broken window. Andy had winded himself with his awkward fall and his right ankle was starting to ache, but he hardly noticed it as he crawled over to his sister. He felt sick as he looked down at her peaceful face. For one terrible moment he thought he might have killed her.

"Kate? Kate-o!"

Her eyelids didn't even flutter, but he could see now that she was breathing. It was as if she had gone a long way away. Andy had heard of people who went into comas and never woke up again and the fall had been all his clumsy fault. The crumbling beam had just come away in his hands and there was dust everywhere now, lazily coiling up in the sunlight.

Panic rose in Andy's head and he couldn't think straight. He picked up one of Kate's limp hands. It was quite warm and very relaxed. It was as if everything was happening very, very slowly and that, like Kate, he couldn't move. Then he heard busy footsteps down below in the yard and somebody whistling.

Andy crawled over to the window and saw Chauval going past followed by three enormous pigs which were sniffing at the big iron swill bin he was carrying.

"Chauval . . ." Andy croaked.

The small, wrinkled brown face looked up at him and then Chauval's expression changed. He put down the bucket, took off his disreputable ancient knitted cap and wiped it across his forehead.

"You all right, eh?"

"It's Kate. I slipped. I think she's been knocked out, maybe she's . . ." Andy's voice wavered to a halt. Chauval came up the rickety stairs two at a time and his bright little eyes took in the situation at once.

"It was an accident," Andy said, sitting down suddenly and putting his head between his knees. For a moment he thought he really was going to be sick. "But it was all my fault. Kate was just behind me when the beam gave way and I lost my balance. Then part of the roof came down and hit her on the head. But it didn't look as though it hit her very hard. It was all so quick. She's not . . .?"

"She's all right." Chauval was sitting back on his heels, his calloused hand gently holding Kate's wrist. "Her colour's coming back and she's breathing regularly. I've seen accidents like this before and some a great deal worse." His face hardened: lines and lines of still bodies lying under filthy, oil-sodden grey blankets. And he'd been younger then

95

than this strapping lad was now. But that was a different world.

"You're *sure* she'll be all right?" Andy persisted. He and Kate might quarrel and bicker a lot, but he hated seeing her like this.

"She'll be around in a moment," Chauval said. "She may have a bit of a headache, her, but there's no feeling of a bump on her head. She wasn't looking too bright before she fell over. I've never seen such a miserable face as hers."

"She doesn't like it here," Andy said. "Ought we to get a doctor? Take her to the hospital? Call Cousin La Bott?"

"Call away," Chauval said. "She'll tell you the same as me. On a farm there's always accidents, let alone what happens down at the harbour and at sea. Your cousin Louisa's husband drowned at sea, off the Casquet Rocks it was, ten years ago . . ." he went on, knowing that talking calmly would stop the boy getting into even more of a state. "There, look, she's coming round, eh?"

Kate's eyelids fluttered, she gave a deep sigh and then very slowly turned her head and looked up at Chauval. She frowned as though something was bothering her and as if he were a stranger then, slowly, her expression changed and she smiled slightly. He went on holding her hand and patting it, shaking his head at Andy who had clambered to his feet.

"She needs calm for a moment or two," Chauval said. "Don't you, eh?"

Kate tried to nod and winced. She took another deep breath and then said huskily, "What happened? Where's this place?"

"It's your Cousin La Bott's old barn. It's a rackety

place and part of the roof gave way and then Andy slipped and fell and so did you. How's your head, eh?"

"It aches a bit. Not much though really . . ."

Kate put her hand to the graze which was rapidly turning bright red.

"Let's see if you can sit up."

Gently, but firmly, Chauval put his arm round her shoulders and brought her up to a sitting position.

"Wow!" said Kate, blowing out her cheeks. "It's all going round a bit." She blinked her eyes rapidly and then focused on Andy. "Oh, for goodness sake stop looking like a St Bernard dog. I'm OK. What a weird thing to happen. I'll be great in a minute." Kate shut her eyes tightly and then turned to look straight at Chauval. "I know it sounds dotty, but for a moment I thought I saw someone in the barn and I heard someone call out a name as I fell."

"What name?"

"I can't remember. It was foreign. Hine, something like that. Oh, it must be the knock on the head. I'm much better now."

She certainly sounded much more like her old bossy self and all the colour had come back into her face. In fact she looked much better now than she had done before the accident. She was actually smiling too, for the first time since they had come to the island. Her head ached a little, but that didn't matter and she wondered why she'd made such a fuss about coming here and wanting to get away. It wasn't like home, of course, but it wasn't too bad really and then as a shadow raced across the camp site the name came back to her.

"Heine," Kate said to Chauval, "that was the name I thought I heard. But who is Heine? What does it mean?"

It was very quiet in the barn. In the distance there was the soft sound of the sea and, below them, the very definite squealing of the pigs who had turned over the swill bucket and were finishing off its contents. Cousin Louisa came out of the farmhouse with the food for the chickens; a tiny, upright figure picking her way through the rusty criss-cross of barbed wire which was still there round the sides of the camp site. Only now there were no prisoners in their stiff shabby uniforms, but just ordinary people having a holiday in all kinds of tents, with a camp shop and showers and free range eggs from Mrs La Bott who ran the whole site so efficiently.

Chauval patted Kate's hand and shrugged.

"It was a long time ago," he said, "when I was older than you and younger than your brother, eh? And there was a soldier who was here. He used to call me 'Mein Kind', that means child in his language. His name was Heine. Perhaps he wrote his name up somewhere and you saw it. We had better get back to put the kettle on, eh?"

"OK." Kate got to her feet. She felt amazingly cheerful, better than she'd ever felt in her life. Which was amazing as she had hated coming to this place and she'd been zonked on the head AND was starting to have the bruise to prove it. "But let's just have a look at what hit me."

It happened very, very slowly for all of them. There was Andy getting up from his knees and just avoiding hitting his head on a low beam, Chauval dusting straw off his knees and smiling to himself about so many things he had half forgotten, and Cousin Louisa returning from the chickens and looking up at them and then Kate picked up the piece of wood and she began to say something as she twirled it round. Then she stopped.

It was faded now and damaged by mice and damp, but it was still all there: the soldier and his wife and the baby. It was a terrible painting, but there was something about the way the painted faces looked out that made them very alive.

"They were my school paints," Chauval said. "Heine borrowed them from me. And he left me his rations . . ."

The other three were staring at him as though he was completely mad. What was he talking about?

Andy looked totally mystified and massaged his wrenched ankle. Kate leant forward, frowning, but very interested. She didn't hate the island any more. It was as if great banks of clouds and unhappiness were moving away and even her head had stopped aching. Cousin La Bott put down her egg boxes and rather stiffly climbed up to join them. The children looked better, not cross and dull any more. Quite soon they would have to start pulling their weight on the farm. She was not a charitable institution, even if they *were* distant relations.

"Andy," Chauval said, "please to climb up, you, to where the roof is rotten."

Andy lumbered to his feet, almost tripped over and then got to where Chauval was pointing. He was so relieved that Kate-o was OK that he wasn't really worried about anything else. Perhaps tomorrow he could hitch a lift on a fishing boat and sail out to the Casquets?

"And reach up into the beams. Feel for something long and heavy," Chauval said, quietly.

Madame La Bott, Old Louie's daughter, turned to him and said, "Ohé. L'affair va-t-elle?"

"Ohé," Chauval agreed. "I know what is there;

what he hid so long ago. But I never knew *where* it was. We remember Dickon and his mother, Ed Tostevin, Old Louie, my parents, Eric and Heine. All gone, but we remember, don't we, eh?"

"There is something here, but it's all wrapped up," Andy said. "And it smells a bit. How did you know it was there and what *is* it, anyway?"

Kate looked out of the window and suddenly she felt happier than she had done in a long time. She was really going to have a wonderful time here and she couldn't, for the life of her, imagine why she'd hated it all so much. There weren't any shadows here and it was a lot more interesting than Alton Towers. You could go anywhere, explore, perhaps even go off on a fishing boat across to France. She wasn't frightened or cold any more. It was like coming home.

"I know what it is," Chauval said, quietly. He unwrapped it very, very slowly. It was almost as hard as iron now but it was still perfect. He shut his eyes tight for a moment.

"Ohé," Chauval said. "The wooden gun." Chiselled in small letters across the butt was "Mein Kind". He turned to look at the tiny upright figure of Madame La Bott. A faint smile crossed her face and she shook her head.

"Yes, yes," she said, "the plaything of a child many years ago. But now it's time for supper. And *after* that, Chauval, you can tell my young relations about its history. But now will you please all move yourselves! Kate, come down slowly. Andy, carry the painting. Val, you bring the gun . . ."

Chauval nodded and, with absolute precision, presented arms – "One, two, three. Stand easy." Then he followed the others down the rickety steps.

HAUNTINGS by Hippo Books is a new series of excellent ghost stories for older readers.

Ghost Abbey by Robert Westall
When Maggie and her family move into a run-down old abbey, they begin to notice some very strange things going on in the rambling old building. Is there any truth in the rumour that the abbey is haunted?

Don't Go Near the Water by Carolyn Sloan
Brendan knew instinctively that he shouldn't go near Blackwater Lake. Especially that summer, when the water level was so low. But what was the dark secret that lurked in the depths of the lake?

Voices by Joan Aiken
Julia had been told by people in the village that Harkin House was haunted. And ever since moving in to the house for the summer, she'd been troubled by violent dreams. What had happened in the old house's turbulent past?

The Nightmare Man by Tessa Krailing
Alex first sees the man of his darkest dreams at Stackfield Pond. And soon afterwards he and his family move in to the old house near the pond — End House — and the nightmare man becomes more than just a dream.

A Wish at the Baby's Grave by Angela Bull
Desperate for some money, Cathy makes a wish for some at the baby's grave in the local cemetery. Straight afterwards, she finds a job at an old bakery. But there's something very strange about the bakery and the two Germans who work there. . .

The Bone-Dog by Susan Price
Susan can hardly believe her eyes when her uncle Bryan makes her a pet out of an old fox-fur, a bone and some drops of blood — and then brings it to life. It's wonderful to have a pet which follows her every command — until the bone-dog starts to obey even her unconscious thoughts. . .

All on a Winter's Day by Lisa Taylor
Lucy and Hugh wake up suddenly one wintry morning to find everything's changed — their mother's disappeared, the house is different, and there are two ghostly children and their evil-looking aunt in the house. What has happened?

The Old Man on a Horse by Robert Westall
Tobias couldn't understand what was happening. His parents and little sister had gone to Stonehenge with the hippies, and his father was arrested. Then his mother disappeared. But while sheltering with his sister in a barn, he finds a statue of an old man on a horse, and Tobias and Greta find themselves transported to the time of the Civil War. . .

The Rain Ghost by Garry Kilworth
What is the secret of the old, rusty dagger Steve finds while on a school expedition? As soon as he brings it home, the ancient-looking knife is connected with all sorts of strange happenings. And one night Steve sees a shadowy, misty figure standing in the pouring rain, watching the house . . .

The Haunting of Sophie Bartholomew by Elizabeth Lindsay
Sophie hates the house she and her mother have moved to in Castle Street. It's cold and dark and very frightening. And when Sophie hears that it's supposed to be haunted, she decides to investigate . . .

Picking Up the Threads by Ian Strachan
There's something strange going on at the rambling old house where Nicky is spending her holidays with her great-aunt. In the middle of the night, Nicky is woken up by the sound of someone crying for help. But when she goes to investigate, there's nobody there!

The Wooden Gun by Elizabeth Beresford
Kate is very unhappy on the Channel Island where she's spending her summer holidays. She senses a mysterious, forbidding atmosphere, but no one else seems to notice it. Is it just her imagination, or does the beautiful, sun-drenched island hide a dark secret?

The Devil's Cauldron by David Wiseman
Although Clare is blind, she lives her life to the full, and is never afraid of taking chances. So when she is told about the old smuggler's cave, she persuades her friend Ned to come with her to explore it. But the cave holds more than just memories of the violence it saw many years ago . . .

STREAMERS

We've got lots of great books for younger readers in Hippo's STREAMERS series:

Sally Ann – On Her Own by Terrance Dicks   £1.75
Sally Ann is a very special toy. She's a rag doll who likes to be involved in everything that's going on. When Sally Ann finds out that the nursery school where she lives might be closed down, she decides it's time to take action!

Sally Ann – The School Play by Terrance Dicks £1.75
When the nursery school's electricity goes off, Sally Ann comes up with a wonderful idea to pay for the new wiring. But not everything runs as smoothly as Sally Ann would like!

The Little Yellow Taxi and His Friends
by Ruth Ainsworth   £1.75
The little grey car can't get to sleep at night, and keeps all the other cars and lorries awake. So the garage owner paints the little car yellow, gives him a sign for his roof, and turns him into an all-night taxi.

Tom by Ruth Silvestre   £1.75
The circus has come to town, and Tom tries to tell his parents about it. But they are always too busy to listen. . . A delightful collection of stories about Tom, his family and friends.

Look out for these other titles in the STREAMERS series:

Nate the Great by Marjorie Sharmat
Nate the Great and the Missing Key by Marjorie Sharmat